LIES

LIES

Even love has its casualties

VANESSA D. WERTS

HIGHER REALM
PUBLISHING

LIES

Published by Higher Realm Publishing

This book is a work of fiction. Names, characters, places, and incidents, are the product of the author's imagination and are not to be construed as real. Any resemblance to actual events, locales, or persons, living or dead, is coincidental.

Higher Realm Publishing
P.O. Box 4632
Ashburn, VA 20148

Printed in the United States of America

Scripture quotations marked NLT are taken from the *Holy Bible*, New Living Translation, copyright 1996, 2004, 2007 by Tyndale House Foundation. Used by permission of Tyndale House Publishers, Inc., Carol Stream, Illinois 60188. All rights reserved.

SECOND EDITION

ISBN: 978-0-692-62766-2
Library of Congress Control Number: 2016901393

Edited by Sarah Norton and Vanessa D. Werts
Cover design by SelfPubBookCovers.com/Daniela
Interior design by Jera Publishing
Author photograph by Picture People
Lyrics by Darryl Omar

To everyone who needs forgiveness...
The love, grace, and mercies of God run deep.

Acknowledgments

God, I love you and thank you for the journey that I had to take in order to pen this novel. It wasn't easy, but you are faithful. I exalt your name!

To Darryl and Deven, my awesome sons: I love you. Thank you for needing me. So much of my maturity has come from being a mother. I wouldn't be me without you.

To the woman who birthed me, cheers louder than anyone for me, and encourages me in everything I do: Joyce Bates. I love you, ma. I'm so grateful to have you as an example of how to fight the good fight of faith.

To my brother, Tommy Bates: thank you for stimulating conversation and for taking an interest in my writing. Much love to you, Gilda, Tommy Jr., and Khory!

To Kara Brooks and Toni Patrick: thank you three times over for proofreading the story early on and providing feedback. Your comments helped me tremendously and I am forever grateful for your input and constant encouragement. Love you ladies!

To Carolyn Oredugba, my sister-friend: I love you mucho grande! Thank you for being a good friend. We can talk about anything and go anywhere, and it's always a good time. Put on your marketing shoes, girly. The book is finally done!

To the sisterhood at my nine to five: thank you for the lively conversations about men and relationships, and for being transparent and vulnerable. I love you to pieces!

To everyone that prays for me: thank you. The Lord bless you and keep you!

To my brothers and sisters in the Christian faith: thank you in advance for not judging the story before getting to the end (see Luke 7:47-50). Much love!

To the reader: this is my baby—my labor of love. I hope you connect with the characters and they make you laugh, think, cry, choose sides, and even get mad. And I hope you become a fan.

Peace in all things,
Vanessa

Chapter 1

Bobbi stood by and watched an airport security agent ramble through her Gucci handbag. The agent had questioned her about a six-ounce bottle of facial moisturizer, which she'd paid fifty dollars for, and then threw it away. When he cleared her to travel, she gathered her belongings—and her dignity—and headed for her boarding gate.

She checked the time and stopped at a café on the departure gate concourse for a vanilla latte. Moving forward in line, she ordered, swiped her card, and then stepped aside. At the condiments bar, she noticed a handsome man stirring his coffee before a deep male voice called out her order for pick up. She gave the stranger a small smile, taking a sip of the smooth steamy beverage to avoid further eye contact, and moved on.

At the boarding gate, Bobbi powered on her laptop to take one last look at her presentation. She clicked through the charts reviewing her notes, and rehearsed her pitch. If everything went according to plan, she would be signing her first professional athlete to the roster at My Way Communications.

Representing a major athlete would give her the exposure she wanted in the world of professional sports. This would diversify her client portfolio and set her up for long-term success. Bobbi smiled.

"United Airlines flight 1507 with service to Atlanta now boarding business class and premier members at gate five," said the attendant, pulling Bobbi out of her dreamy state.

She put away her laptop, drank the last of her latte, and then went to stand near the blue ropes for boarding.

That's when she saw the attractive man from the café ahead of her with a tall model-type chick at his side. Bobbi couldn't deny how well he wore his jeans and the way his muscles rippled underneath the white polo shirt. Hmmm. She wondered if they were a couple. And just before handing the attendant his boarding pass, the stranger looked back at Bobbi, and she looked away.

When Bobbi boarded, she walked past the interesting couple to her seat and put her carry-on in the overhead compartment. She said a prayer for the flight and for her meeting. She had a lot to be thankful for. After five years in business, Bobbi had managed to position her company as one of the leading independent public relations agencies in Washington, DC. And signing a star athlete like Terry Barnes would take her business to the next level.

In Atlanta, Bobbi deplaned and followed the signs to ground transportation. The stranger and his companion were just ahead of her. Who was this guy anyway? Bobbi frowned. Why did she care?

Eyeing the restroom sign ahead to her right, Bobbi took a detour to freshen up for the meeting, and the couple from the plane disappeared down an escalator.

"Good morning. May I help you?" said the woman behind the desk with a cute pixie haircut.

"Yes. Good morning. My name is Bobbi Farqua." Bobbi looked at her watch. "I'm a bit early, but I have a ten-thirty appointment with Mister Kendall."

The receptionist checked the schedule and picked up the phone. "Mister Kendall, your ten-thirty is here."

"Miss Farqua is here?" he said. "Uhh . . . give me about ten minutes. Thanks, Tish."

The receptionist turned her attention back to Bobbi. "Please have a seat. Mister Kendall will be with you shortly."

"Thank you."

Bobbi picked up the June issue of *Black Enterprise* from the glass-top table and sat down. She crossed her legs and flipped through the pages.

Competing with big public relations firms required Bobbi to bring her A-game to every business deal. Stellar customer service and personal attention to detail had been the key to her fast-track success—and that's how she would win over Atlanta Condors' star running back.

"Hi Bobbi. Jim Kendall." He smiled and extended his hand.

Bobbi stood to greet him. "Yes, Jim. How are you? Finally, we meet."

Jim chuckled. "I know. It took many conversations to get to this point. But we're here now. If you're ready, let's go back to my office."

Bobbi grabbed her things and followed Jim out of the reception area through another set of glass doors and down a hallway. They chatted about her flight on the way to his office.

"By the way, thanks again for sending a driver," said Bobbi.

"No problem. I'm glad it worked out for you. I'll call Eugene after the meeting so he can take you wherever you want to go while—"

The phone rang, interrupting them as they entered Jim's office. He moved quickly around his desk to answer it and motioned for Bobbi to have a seat.

"Yes, Tish?"

"Terry called and said he'll be up after he finds parking."

"Okay. Send him back when he gets here."

Bobbi admired the mahogany furniture in Jim's office while she waited. When Jim got off the phone, he went to sit on the corner of his desk near Bobbi and they continued talking about her visit. When Terry made it to Jim's office, he knocked once and entered.

"What's up, man?" said Terry, moving toward Jim.

"Hey there, man. Glad you could make it," said Jim, greeting Terry with a handshake and man-hug. "This is Bobbi Farqua, the publicist I've been talking to you about." Then Jim said, "Bobbi, meet Terry 'Sweet Feet' Barnes, star running back for the Atlanta Condors."

Terry extended his hand. "A pleasure to meet you, Miss Farqua."

Bobbi stood, reaching for Terry's hand and smiled. "Please call me Bobbi. The pleasure is all mine, Sweet Feet." She chuckled. "Thanks for taking the time to meet with me."

Terry brought Bobbi's hand to his lips and kissed it. She almost gagged when his wet lips pressed against her skin. This wasn't the professional reception she'd expected, but whatever. Jim cleared his throat.

"Hey, guys," said Jim. "Let's move to the conference room and get started."

Once there, Jim and Terry sat at the table and chatted while Bobbi prepared for her presentation. She opened her laptop and plugged it into a portable projector to display her presentation on the white board. Then she walked to the front of the table opposite her audience and began her pitch.

For the next twenty minutes, Bobbi talked about her agency's capabilities. She talked about new endorsement deals and ideas for expanding the Sweet Feet brand with Nike. When Bobbi mentioned getting Terry an exclusive deal with a popular sports-drink company, Terry and Jim both nodded their approval, eagerly awaiting her next word.

Bobbi walked toward the gentlemen as she concluded the meeting. "So you see, Terry, at My Way Communications, we take charge of every situation. We tell the story—the story doesn't tell us." With her final words, Bobbi sat next to Sweet Feet. "You have any questions for me?"

"I'm impressed," said Terry. "Do you represent any other professional athletes?"

"You mean besides you?" She chuckled. "Just kidding. You would be my first. However," she reached in her bag and pulled out a folder, "here's a list of my clients. They've agreed to talk with you about their experience at My Way."

Terry reached for the file. "Thanks." He looked at Jim.

"Here," said Bobbi, handing Terry a business card. "Take your time and check out my company and my credentials. And when you're ready, give me a call."

Bobbi shut down her equipment while Terry read over her client list and Jim made small talk with her about the meeting.

A few minutes later, Terry stood to excuse himself. But before he left the room, he thanked Bobbi for coming to Atlanta. "I'll definitely be in touch," he said, kissing her hand again. "Safe travels." He winked at her and walked out.

Bobbi held back a frown. Rumor had it that Terry was engaged, so she didn't appreciate his flirty eyes or his wet lips. She wanted his business—not him.

As Bobbi finished packing her things, Jim watched her every move.

"So, Bobbi," he said, "I may have some other business to throw your way, if you're interested. I like your style. From what I just saw here, Terry should be ready to sign on the dotted line today. You convinced me . . . and if I need to convince him, I will."

"Thanks for the vote of confidence," she said, zipping her bag. "I'm sure Terry will make the right decision for him. But as for your other clients, give me a call and we can go from there."

"Sounds good to me." Jim used the telephone in the conference room to call for the car and escorted Bobbi back to the reception area.

"Thanks for setting up the meeting . . . and for the car," said Bobbi. "I look forward to working with you." She shook Jim's hand. "Enjoy the rest of your day."

Chapter 3

B obbi pondered the meeting with Terry. Closing this deal had been her primary focus for weeks. She had expected him to make a decision before she left Jim's office.

When she'd talked with Jim in the weeks leading up to the meeting, she learned that Terry had been through a number of publicists over the years. And this time around, he wanted to be the top priority and not just another client on a list, so they were considering smaller firms.

Nevertheless, Bobbi had to trust that all the work she'd put into signing Terry would pay off. So, she pushed aside her speculating thoughts and called her mother when the driver got off the exit for Buckhead.

"Hello."

"Hey, Ma! What are you doing?"

"Hey there, baby girl. I'm in my office, working. You on your way?"

"Yep. Should be there in fifteen minutes," said Bobbi.

"Okay. See you when you get here. Be safe."

When Bobbi arrived at her mother's house, she put her key in the door and before she could close it, Grace met her in the foyer. They hugged and planted butterfly kisses on each other's cheeks, and then doted over hair, clothes, skin, and make-up—the usual girly stuff—like they hadn't seen one another in years.

They went to the kitchen and Grace poured Bobbi a glass of iced tea. Grace asked about the meeting and Bobbi told her that she felt good about the pitch but hadn't closed the deal just yet. They chatted a while longer about family matters and Grace's plans for the summer before a rumbling in Bobbi's stomach reminded her that she hadn't eaten today. And she knew exactly where she wanted to go—Leonard's Grille on Peachtree Road. So the mother and daughter jumped in Grace's red two-seater convertible Benz and headed to lunch.

At Leonard's Grille, they ordered, and once the server left the table, Grace asked Bobbi if she'd contacted Lance. Bobbi rolled her eyes. She knew her mom wouldn't let this day go by without asking about him.

"No, Ma. I haven't had time to show him around, so I haven't reached out yet."

"He's a very nice, successful young man. He's going to think I lied to his mother about my wonderful, kind-hearted daughter. I wish you would just call the man."

"I will." Bobbi shrugged her shoulders. "When I get a chance."

"Okay, dear. Now, don't lie to your mother. You know I don't play."

Grace's phone rang and Bobbi breathed a sigh of relief. She didn't want to go back and forth with her mom, or talk about this Lance guy. She would get around to meeting him soon. Things were busy at work and Bobbi didn't need any new male friends—and certainly not a friend of her mother's.

Besides, Grace had mentioned that Lance was a single parent, and that made Bobbi uncomfortable. What if he or his child got attached to her? The thought of it made her cringe. Bobbi ate her salmon and scrolled through work emails while Grace took the call.

After lunch, the two were able to get in some retail therapy before Bobbi's flight. They stopped in a designer boutique and then strolled by a couple of shoe stores before Grace dragged Bobbi into a hobby store looking for jewelry beads. She made them matching bracelets while they sat in front of Fairview Tower waiting for Eugene to take Bobbi back to the airport.

The bumper-to-bumper traffic on Interstate 85 South made Bobbi grateful once again that Jim had provided a car. She should be at the airport in thirty minutes—an hour and a half before her flight.

Bobbi kicked off her heels and wiggled her toes, wondering what her man was doing. She chuckled. Tony could never be her man—he loved women too much. But she had to give him props for how well he played the role of convenient lover. Whenever her libido needed attention, he always came through with no questions asked. And after all she'd been through today—she could use a release.

Bobbi's phone rang.

"What's up, Nikki?" she said.

"Hey, B. You know why I'm calling, so give it up. How'd the meeting with Sweet Feet go?"

Bobbi smiled. "You know I did my thing. I'm just waiting for a yes."

"Is he fine in person?" said Nikki.

"Yeah, but dude is super duper weird though . . . almost inappropriate—" Bobbi's phone beeped. "Hey, let me call you back. Got a business call coming in."

Bobbi hung up with Nikki and accepted the incoming call from Jim Kendall.

"Hello, Bobbi Farqua," she said.

"Bobbi. This is Jim. Are you at the airport?"

"Hey, Jim. Not yet, but we're getting there."

"Great. I talked with Terry after you left and he has a few questions for you."

"Sure. Is he there with you now?" Bobbi said.

"No . . . he left not long after you did this morning."

"Okay. Well, I'll have my assistant call your office first thing tomorrow morning to arrange a conference call."

"Sounds great. Have a safe flight."

"Thank you. Bye."

Bobbi pumped her fist in the air. Signing Terry would happen—it had to. She shifted on the soft leather seat and squeezed her thighs together. Something about closing big business deals toyed with her hormones. Maybe the sense of fulfillment in her work caused her body to react this way. Or perhaps it had to do with an adrenaline rush. Whatever the case, the familiar twitch down below demanded action.

After Bobbi checked in for her flight and escaped airport security, she pulled out her phone and called Tony.

"Hey, love," he answered.

"Hey, you. Can you come over tonight?"

"Uhh . . . yeah."

"Cool." Bobbi checked the time. "Eleven-thirty is good. And, oh—" she giggled. "Don't wear any underwear. I don't want anything in my way."

"You just be ready when I get there."

———※●●———

Onboard the plane, Bobbi fastened her seatbelt and closed her eyes. Her lips turned up in a smile. Finally, she could get some sleep.

"Excuse me. Is that seat taken? Miss . . . excuse me," said the man standing in the aisle. "Is anyone sitting there?"

Bobbi's eyes popped open. In the aisle next to her, pointing at the window seat stood the mystery man from her morning flight. She had to be dreaming.

Bobbi poked her chest. "You talking to me?"

"Yes. Is that seat taken . . . the window seat?"

Bobbi looked around at the other vacant seats nearby, wondering what seat number he had on his boarding pass. "Uh . . . I don't know."

He proceeded to secure his belongings and side stepped past her to the window seat.

Bobbi forced a smile and nodded in his direction. Then she closed her eyes again and pressed her head against the seat— thoughts of Tony slowly fading into the shadow of curiosity with her new travel companion.

Once he settled in, the mystery man pulled out his phone and made a call. Bobbi didn't want to eavesdrop, but she couldn't help her self. Based on the tone of his voice, he had to be talking to a woman. And the unmistakable way he said, "I love you" before ending the call, told Bobbi all she needed to know.

While the flight attendant prepared the cabin for takeoff, Bobbi cut her eye at Mr. What's-his-name sitting to her left. Game recognized game. He'd indirectly made a full disclosure about his current status, just in case the two of them became acquainted on the flight.

Bobbi went to the restroom after the pilot announced the altitude and turned off the fasten seatbelt light. When she returned to her seat, the handsome stranger at the window took the opportunity to introduce himself.

"By the way, my name is Savon—Savon Turner." He extended his hand. "Weren't you on the flight this morning?"

Checkmate. Bobbi reached across the center seat to shake his hand.

"Hi, Savon, nice to meet you. I'm Bobbi Farqua. And yes, I do remember you from this morning." Savon's hand held hers longer than she'd expected, considering the phone call she'd just heard.

After introductions, an awkward silence filled the space between them. Bobbi was curious, but not desperate. If he didn't say another word the entire flight, neither would she.

"So . . . Bobbi. Are you from DC?" said Savon, interrupting her thought.

"No. I was raised in Atlanta—in Buckhead. But I live in the DC area," she said.

"Small world. What part of Buckhead?" said Savon.

"Peachtree Park."

"Me too—on the north side. My family moved there from New York when I was in high school," he said.

"No way," said Bobbi. "Humph. You don't look familiar."

"You either," he said.

They talked about their neighborhoods and growing up in the A. When they started name-dropping, they discovered they knew some of the same people.

"Talk about coincidences," said Bobbi.

"Yeah . . ." Savon gazed at her. "Do you follow pro sports?"

"A little. I usually go to a few games—football and basketball."

"Hmmm," he said.

Then Bobbi added, "But I like basketball more, cause the Washington Warriors football team sucks."

Savon frowned. "I play for the Warriors. I just did a radio interview and an autograph signing at my old high school."

A brunette flight attendant with red lipstick on her front tooth interrupted their conversation. "Would you like something to drink?" she said.

Both Savon and Bobbi asked for water and the attendant scribbled on a pad and moved on.

"Don't get me wrong," Bobbi said. "I definitely consider myself a Warriors fan, but come on—you guys could do much better." She giggled. "My girlfriend and I say the team should try exorcism to cast out that losing demon. Ha!" Bobbi held her chest to quiet the laughter.

When she realized her humor had offended Savon, she changed the subject to smooth things over. To answer one of his earlier questions, she told him that she was a publicist. They talked about her line of work and about making money in general. When the flight attendant rolled by with their waters and two bags of honey-roasted peanuts, Bobbi took the opportunity to shift the conversation again.

She asked him about his social life and where he hung out. The exchange between them flowed with little to no effort and, before long the pilot interrupted the cabin with an announcement to prepare for landing.

In the time it took to fly from Atlanta to DC, the chemistry between them grew. But Savon had already told Bobbi that he had a fiancée. So she knew their meeting today would be both the beginning and the end of her curiosity. Although Bobbi didn't want a serious relationship, she never wanted to be the one to help a cheater cheat.

As the plane landed, neither one said a word. In their silence, thoughts flooded Bobbi's mind about meeting the perfect stranger.

The two exited the aircraft and walked down the concourse and out to the parking garage together. Then things became awkward again. Had Savon not been engaged, Bobbi would know what to say to keep him on the hook. But that wasn't the case.

She flipped her hair over her shoulder and reached in her purse for a business card. "If you're ever in the market for a publicist, give me a call," she said, handing him the card.

He examined it and looked at her. "You didn't say you owned a PR agency." He tapped the card against his finger. "Hmmm. I'm impressed. Brains and beauty."

Bobbi looked up at Savon and, when their eyes met, she knew she had to leave. "Well, it's been a long day. My bed is calling me. It was a pleasure meeting you though, and reminiscing about home—"

"Check it out," he interrupted, "a few of my homeboys are coming to DC to hang out with me this weekend. We'll be at Club Dream, Friday night. You should come."

Bobbi tried not to read into his invite. She turned to press the elevator button and then looked back at him. "If I can, me and my girl will stop by for drinks," Bobbi lied. Thank goodness for the ding of the elevator—she needed to get far away from this man. "Take care, Savon," said Bobbi before the doors closed.

Chapter 4

B obbi checked the water temperature before stopping up the tub, and then added lavender bath crystals. Tea-light candles burned throughout the house as Maxwell crooned "This Woman's Work" over the speakers. For reasons she couldn't explain, the song made her feel sexy.

She pinned up her hair with a clip and stepped into the sudsy water. The melodic waves of the neo-soul artist's falsetto filled the house. Tony hated this song because she played it almost every time he came over. He would say, "Who plays the same freakin' song in repeat mode for hours?" Bobbi laughed.

She took her time cleansing the grit from two climates off of her body. After drying off, she smoothed on a citrusy body lotion and went to find something to wear. Flipping through her lingerie drawer, Bobbi pulled out a tiny black lace thong and grinned.

Then she scanned the boxes of shoes in her closet—all of which had pictures taped in front—and chose a pair of strappy black heels. Humming along to her favorite song, she applied just a little mascara and lip-gloss and released her hair from the clip, bringing long black locks cascading down to rest over her breasts. Her eyes twinkled. Perfect.

Bobbi tidied her room and headed downstairs to the kitchen in nothing but a thong and her heels. She took the bubbly out of the freezer and grabbed two flutes from the cupboard. The doorbell rang just as Bobbi uncorked the bottle. She filled the glasses and went to open the door.

"Hey, babe," Bobbi said, handing Tony a glass. She reached for his free hand and pulled him inside.

"B." Tony let his overnight bag slide from his shoulder. "You're beautiful."

He set his champagne on the table near the door and pulled Bobbi to him. He kissed her slow at first, then the kisses became more hungry. He backed her against the wall, his mouth doing most of the work from her lips to her breast to her belly—and then to that spot, giving Bobbi her first release of the evening. Then she unzipped his pants and reached inside for what she wanted. The corners of her lips turned up at the stiff promise of uninhibited hours of pleasure, and she led him over to the sofa to get the party started.

⟶➤●◄⟵

On Saturday morning, Bobbi lay in bed, reflecting over the events of the past week. Yesterday, the fruits of her labor had finally paid off with Terry Barnes. He'd come to town on other business and had stopped by her office to sign the paperwork. Afterwards they had gone to lunch, and she learned more about him on a personal level. He'd confirmed his engagement, but also told Bobbi that she could call him if she needed anything—emphasizing the word "anything." Sweet Feet seemed like a decent guy for the most part, but he had one concussion too many if he thought there would be anything between them besides business. Bobbi shook her head. Yet another man she had to school about testing her boundaries.

She rolled over and looked at the clock. Then her thoughts went to Jim Kendall. Jim had called on Thursday to set up meetings for a few of his clients. Bobbi appreciated that he'd been consistent and deliberate about them doing business. She hadn't noticed a wedding ring on his finger, but of course that meant nothing in this day and age. Maybe she would check him out when she went to Atlanta in a couple of weeks. It couldn't hurt to get better acquainted.

Next, the image of the Warriors wide receiver she'd met on the plane tickled her brain. Savon, Savon, Savon. Um-um-um. Why were the good ones always taken? But Bobbi couldn't be so sure she'd want a man like Savon for herself. He'd flirted with her far too much to be one step away from the altar. Humph. His fiancée had her hands full.

Last on her radar would be Lance, the guy her mom wanted her to meet. Maybe she would give him a call this weekend to see if he needed anything. She owed it to her mother to call him at least once.

Bobbi stretched and rolled out of bed. She and Nikki had plans for the day, which included breakfast at Nikki's house. So Bobbi showered and dressed and then took the forty-five minute drive into the city. She parked her white CLS 400 Coupe Benz at the curb in front of Nikki's condo and made her way to the third floor and knocked on the door.

"It's open," yelled Nikki.

The smell of buttermilk biscuits and sausage drew Bobbi to the kitchen, where she found Nikki taking a pan from the oven.

"Dang, girl. You're like the master chef in here. Those home-made biscuits?"

"You know it. Just like momma makes 'em. We can't eat Greek yogurt all the time. These southern butts need sustenance."

Bobbi poked hers out. "You have a point."

They both laughed as Nikki put breakfast on the table. Bobbi got the orange juice and apricot preserves from the refrigerator and Nikki blessed the food.

"Do you know Savon Turner? He plays for the Warriors?" said Bobbi, spreading preserves on her biscuit.

"Yeah. He was recently traded from the Condors," said Nikki before biting a sausage. "What about him?"

"He sat next to me on my flight from Atlanta, Monday night. We had the best conversation—he's cool."

"So what's up with the tender voice? You like this guy or something?" said Nikki.

Bobbi chuckled. "My voice is not tender. Nah . . . he's engaged. I just wondered if you'd heard of him."

"Well, you know you can always ask Gavin what he knows," said Nikki. "You know he'll tell you everything." Gavin was Nikki's cousin who also played for the Warriors.

"Nah, I'm good. I told you he's engaged," Bobbi said.

"Okay." Nikki let it go, but she heard the intrigue in her best friend's voice and saw a spark in her eyes.

Bobbi ignored Nikki's questioning stare. She realized Nikki could tell when she was excited about a guy. A few years ago, Bobbi had been in a relationship she thought would lead to marriage. But after two years, a woman and her pregnant belly had knocked on Bobbi's front door, and just like that, her perfect life had unraveled. She'd found out her man had cheated in the worst way possible.

So it didn't matter if she liked Savon or not. She wouldn't put her self in a losing predicament.

Nikki and Bobbi finished breakfast and then narrowed down their choices of things to do for the rest of the day. Bobbi cleaned the kitchen while Nikki got dressed, and thirty minutes later, they were headed out for a day at the spa and shopping.

Chapter 5

A couple of weeks later, Bobbi took Nikki out to celebrate her passing the Maryland State Bar—her second licensing. Bobbi gave her name to the hostess and they went to the bar and ordered drinks while they waited for a table. Bobbi took her glass and turned toward Nikki.

"Here's to you, Attorney Barton," said Bobbi, lifting the watermelon martini. "For persevering, sacrificing, and pressing your way in spite of the odds. I'm very proud of you."

"Aww . . . thank you, boo," said Nikki.

They were at their favorite DC sports bar, Indi Red. The latest R&B played in the background and four, sixty-inch monitors hung in the bar area, broadcasting games from three different sports networks, and the latest from CNN. Bobbi and Nikki chatted and glanced around the room. Coming here never disappointed. It was the happy hour and weekend hangout spot for local celebrities, athletes and young professionals.

When the square buzzer lit up and vibrated in Bobbi's hand, they gulped down the last of their drinks and followed the hostess to their table.

"Your server will be with you shortly," said the hostess as they scooted into the booth.

Both ladies smiled in thanks and picked up a menu. Bobbi ordered fish tacos and Nikki selected the seared tuna with summer vegetables. No biscuits tonight.

During dinner, the two friends giggled like schoolgirls, reminiscent of their childhood. Bobbi and Nikki were more like sisters than best friends. They'd been inseparable since second grade. After high school, Bobbi had gone into the military for four years while Nikki followed her dream to be an attorney. And somehow, with different paths, they'd both ended up right here in the DC area.

Life had worked out for them to support each other through the good and bad times. They were on the front lines for each other—whether cheering, or in the battle—they had each other's backs.

The waitress returned to the table to check on them. "Would you ladies like dessert?"

Bobbi looked at the waitress, and then her eyes darted to follow a couple being seated on the other side of the dining area. She pulled her eyes away from the couple long enough to order Dutch apple pie with vanilla ice cream, and then glanced back at them.

"Oh my," said Bobbi. "You won't believe this. Savon just walked in with his fiancée."

"No way. Where?"

"Over there in the brown shirt. You see him?"

Nikki pointed. "You mean him? Whaatt?" Nikki turned back around then glanced back at him and shook her head."

"What?" Bobbi said.

"I bet his woman has high blood pressure and wet pillowcases." Nikki reached her spoon in Bobbi's dessert. "I'm just sayin'."

Bobbi frowned. "What does that mean?"

Nikki chuckled. "He's just too fine—that's all. There is such a thing you know."

"Whatever, girl." Bobbi licked the back of her spoon. "I think I'll go over and say hello before we leave."

"Why?" said Nikki. "He's with his woman."

"I just want to say hi—that's all."

Nikki agreed with Bobbi that it shouldn't be a big deal for her to go over and speak to the man. But it wasn't the best timing.

Moments later, a group of their friends joined them at the table to surprise Nikki. They all ordered dessert and when they finished eating, they moved the party over to the bar area.

Their party of seven got drinks and huddled at the far right end of the bar. Everyone joked and laughed, enjoying the celebration except for Bobbi. She'd been preoccupied with mustering up the nerve to go over and speak to Savon. It had been almost a month since they'd met on the plane and she wondered how he would act toward her in front of his fiancée. She wanted to see if her presence would affect him.

"Hey, I'm going to the restroom," said Bobbi. "You coming?"

"Nah . . . I'm good," said Nikki.

"Well, hold this for me." Bobbi handed Nikki her drink. "I'll be right back."

The restrooms were halfway between the bar and dining area. When Bobbi turned to walk down the hallway toward the restroom, she saw that Savon was alone at the table. She took the opportunity to go over and speak.

"So, Mister Turner," Bobbi tapped Savon on the shoulder, "how's it going?"

Savon craned his neck to see the face behind the familiar voice. His eyes grew wide when he saw Bobbi. "It's Bobbi, right?" he said.

Bobbi frowned. "Yes, it's Bobbi." She didn't know whether to be angry or pop him upside the head to jar his memory. This joker had talked her ear off on the plane, and now he had brain-fog about her name? Amazing. Disappointed now, Bobbi said, "You dining alone?" Of course she knew the answer, but she needed to bide time to figured out her exit strategy. She didn't want to look even more foolish by running off.

"Nah. My fiancée is here."

"Oh. Okay."

Just then, Bobbi looked over her shoulder and saw Miss Lady walking toward the table. For the sport of it, and because Savon had just irritated the heck out of her, Bobbi stuck around to see how he would handle the situation.

The look on his fiancée's face challenged Bobbi and her purpose for being at their table. She sat down without acknowledging Bobbi's presence.

Savon grabbed her hand. "Babe, this is Bobbi Farqua. She's a publicist." Then he looked at Bobbi. "And Bobbi, this is my fiancée, Monica."

"Hello, Monica." Bobbi extended her hand.

"How do you know her?" Monica said to Savon, dismissing Bobbi.

"Uh, we met a few weeks ago," he said.

Bobbi couldn't believe Monica's disrespect. She had to separate herself from this nonsense before it got out of hand.

"Well you two . . . have a good night." With a less than genuine smile, Bobbi nodded and left.

On Monday morning, Bobbi entered her office building with purpose. Four-inch stilettos and a rolling bag filled with files she'd taken home over the weekend didn't slow her down one bit. She pressed the button at the elevator, cutting her eye at the gentleman in a suit and tie that walked up beside her.

"Good morning," he said.

Bobbi looked over at him and forced a smile. "Hi."

She didn't say another word. Bobbi was still irritated about Savon and his rude fiancée. At the very least, she had expected him to be cordial. But instead, he had been cold and indifferent.

The elevator opened and the gentleman motioned for Bobbi to step in ahead of him. She entered and pressed three. The gentleman pressed five—the top floor of the building. There were only two businesses on the top level: an IT firm and a sports agency. And, judging from the muscles protruding from his too-tight suit coat, Bobbi figured him to be an athlete headed to the sports agency. Humph. Like she cared.

The doors opened on three and Bobbi exited. The gentleman called out to her, "Enjoy your day."

"Thank you," she said, looking over her shoulder with a fake smile.

Today, and for most of the week, Bobbi would be doing damage control for her most needy client, Lil Dizzy. The young hip-hop rapper had raw talent, but he couldn't keep his mouth shut or his hands to himself. For example, the celebrity gossip website Bobbi perused right now, claimed that Dizzy had been at a nightclub over the weekend, spewing negative comments about another rapper. The media loved reporting on his bad behavior. However, under his tough façade, Bobbi saw something more. She recognized his good manners and gentle spirit whenever she met with him in person, and that compelled her to continue to fight for his image.

"Excuse me, Bobbi," said Ciara, Bobbi's assistant. She stood in the doorway of Bobbi's office. "Are you still going to DC to meet Nikki for lunch?"

Bobbi looked up from her work. "I didn't realize it was noon. No, I'll be here for lunch. My schedule just went off the rails."

"You want me to call Nikki?" said Ciara.

"No, I'll do it. Thanks."

Bobbi called Nikki to cancel their lunch date and learned that Nikki had been swamped too and couldn't make it. So they chatted a few minutes and then hung up.

By the time Bobbi finished for the day, it was almost 9:00 PM. She closed down the office and headed out. When she made it to her car parked at the curb, the driver's side front tire had a flat. She threw up her hands, looking around and hoping that someone might be near to help, but then thought better of it.

Shaking her head, she opened the car door and threw her purse and briefcase in the backseat. Then she took her cell phone and walked back toward the office building. Good thing she'd parked under a streetlight.

When she got closer to the building, she noticed a man standing in the lobby through the glass doors. It startled her at first, but she knew some old military defense tactics she could use if necessary.

But when she entered the building, she recognized the gentleman from earlier that morning.

"Hi there. Everything okay?" he said.

"Uh . . . hi. Not really," said Bobbi. "I have a flat tire."

"Let me take a look. I can put your spare on, so you can make it home."

"That would be really nice," Bobbi admitted, breathing a sigh of relief.

He smiled and extended his hand. "My name is Lance— Lance Holder."

Lance. *Hmmm*. "Nice to meet you, Lance. I'm Bobbi." She shook his hand. "I have to ask . . . are you following me today? This is my second time running into you." Bobbi laughed. If he had been following her, she was perfectly fine with it right now.

Lance laughed, too. "No, Bobbi, I'm not following you. But I could ask you the same thing."

"I can assure you," said Bobbi, "I don't have time to follow anyone."

They laughed together and walked outside to her car. Lance checked the tire, but couldn't tell what had punctured it. He asked her to pop the trunk while he peeled off his tight jacket. She had wondered how he would manage to do it all in that second-skin.

Lance didn't talk much while he changed the tire, other than to answer Bobbi's questions. She asked if he worked in the building since he was there so late—and he said, yes. She also wanted to know why he wore his clothes so tight, but instead of asking she just chuckled to herself.

After he tightened the last lug nut, he put the flat tire in her trunk and she handed him back his jacket.

"Thank you so much for helping me," said Bobbi.

"No problem. It was my pleasure. What kind of man would I be if I left a beautiful lady stranded?" Lance threw his jacket over his shoulder.

"Here's my card." He reached in his wallet. "If something happens on your way home, give me a call."

"Thank you." Bobbi took the card and smiled.

He opened her car door. "I have to get home myself," he said. "Be safe."

At home, Bobbi showered and got in bed. What a day. Sitting with her back against the red upholstered headboard, she picked up Lance's business card. He was the owner of Holder Enterprises. Lance had mentioned that he had an IT business on the fifth floor of the building while he changed her flat.

He had to be the same Lance her mother kept talking about. So, Bobbi scrolled to the text message from her mom back in January that had his contact information. Bingo. The numbers matched.

Nevertheless, Bobbi wasn't ready to let Lance know that she was Grace's daughter. Although she didn't doubt that Lance had already figured that out. How embarrassing and ironic for them to meet this way. But if he didn't say anything, neither would she. Not yet, at least.

Lance seemed like a nice guy and she could appreciate that he hadn't said anything inappropriate or tried to hit on her tonight. Bobbi yawned and put the card on the nightstand—tomorrow she would sleep in before heading to work. But before she turned off the lamp, she got on her knees to pray. The flat tire aside, she had to count her many blessings.

Lord, thank you for today . . . for helping me get through it with a good attitude. Savon really ticked me off the other night, but I pulled myself together. And what's her name . . . yeah, Monica . . . I had some choice words for her, but you helped me with that too. And thank you God for letting Lance stay late to help me with the flat. Only you could have orchestrated that. I love you! Amen.

Chapter 6

A private, preseason party for the Warriors had everyone in town wanting an invite. Bobbi had declined Nikki's plus-one invitation from Gavin at first, thinking she and Tony would get together. But her plans fell through and she didn't want to spend July fourth watching the fireworks on television alone, so she called Nikki.

"Hey, Nikki. I changed my mind about the party."

"Well now," said Nikki. "Your change of heart wouldn't have anything to do with a certain gentleman you met on an aero-plane, would it?"

Bobbi sucked her teeth. "Forget Savon. I changed my mind because I don't have anything else to do. Plus, everyone I know is going, so I may as well network."

Nikki laughed. "Call Gavin and let him know."

"Okay. Let me get back to work," said Bobbi. "I'll let you know what he says."

Saturday night, the line to get in the party was wrapped around the building. When Bobbi and Nikki arrived, they maneuvered through the crowd standing near the doorway, and the bouncer removed the velvet rope for them to enter the club.

Club Dream had five levels with different genres of music playing on each. On the ground level, folks were dancing to salsa, while jazz played on the second floor. But on the third level, it was time to party or go home. Every square foot of the dance floor had happy feet gliding across it. Even the DJ pumped his fist from where he stood, elevated above the crowd.

"Ooh . . . that's my jam," said Nikki. "Come on, B, let's go dance."

Nikki grabbed Bobbi's arm and they worked their way through the crowded dance floor. She chose a spot next to a football player they both knew. He moved from side to side like a robot, whispering in his dance partner's ear. Bobbi and Nikki squeezed the lame couple out of their space, just like they had at parties back in their early twenties.

Tonight, the two friends danced together like they were ten years old again. They did the whip and nae-nae, and even took a trip down memory lane with some of the old favorites, like the prep and the snake. It was tempting to drop-it-like-it's-hot, but this wasn't the place or the crowd for that. Even so, it was the most fun they'd had in a long time.

"There's Gavin," Bobbi said, pointing across the room.

Nikki turned to look. "Oh, I see him. Let's go see what that fool is up to."

When they reached Gavin, three women in micro mini-dresses were entertaining him.

"Uhh, what's up, cuz?" said Nikki.

"Yo! What's up?" said Gavin, excusing himself from the ladies and stepping in to hug Nikki.

"So I guess you don't see me standing here?" said Bobbi with her hands on her hips.

"Come here, girl, with yo fine self." He reached for Bobbi's arm. "Give big daddy some love." Gavin had a serious crush on Bobbi when they were kids, but she always treated him like a brother.

"Shut up, boy." Bobbi laughed and hugged him back. She was four years his senior and knew too much about him to take anything he said seriously.

Nikki smacked her lips. "Can a sister get a drink or what?"

"So I'm the bartender now?" said Gavin. He turned his hat sideways. "What y'all drinking?"

He kissed Bobbi on the cheek then went to the bar. After he returned, Bobbi and Nikki moved on to check out the VIP rooms on the fourth and fifth levels. When Nikki ran into a friend from school, Bobbi excused herself and continued working her way through the club.

She walked out onto the rooftop where torches burned and white linens were suspended as canopies over the seating areas. This party had been the perfect outing to get her mind off of work and to just relax. Humming along to the R&B ballad playing in the background, Bobbi sipped her drink while looking over the terrace. A soft tap came on her shoulder and she turned around.

"Hey there," said Savon, pushing his hands down in his pants pockets.

Humph. Bobbi wanted to ignore this clown, but she didn't. "Hello, Savon." Her smile was genuine but guarded. She didn't want any drama tonight.

Savon shifted on his feet. "Look, Bobbi. I owe you an apology for how things went down at the restaurant. Monica can be jealous, but she didn't mean anything by it."

Bobbi looked up at Savon. What a weak excuse. It had been his behavior that had surprised her, not Monica's. "Personally," she said, "I thought the whole episode was a bit much, but you don't have to apologize to me for her behavior. It is what it is."

"So we're good?" he said.

"Of course." But Bobbi was finished with the conversation. "It was good seeing you again. Take care." She stepped past him and went to look for Nikki.

<hr/>

With the first preseason game only days away, Savon found it difficult to stay focused. Monica badgered him about Bobbi every chance she got. She didn't like the way Bobbi had interrupted their intimate dinner at Indi Red two months ago and wouldn't let it go. Monica believed that Bobbi had waited for her to leave the table and then pounced on her man. In Monica's opinion, Bobbi couldn't be trusted.

Savon tried to look at things from Monica's perspective because he loved her and they had a future together. But he didn't think Bobbi meant any harm that night, so the nonsense had to stop. Thank goodness Monica hadn't relocated to DC with him when he got traded. Savon could tolerate her bad attitude in small doses when she visited. But lately, even the short stays had been challenging for him at best.

Nevertheless, the Bobbi drama couldn't compare to the troubles that had surfaced in his life last week. This chick named LaShawn had Savon stressed out about a paternity issue. LaShawn had been blowing up his phone accusing him of being the father of her two-year-old son. Savon didn't know how long he could keep it a secret from Monica, or how long it would be before LaShawn went to the media with her story. She seemed determined to make him the father and refused to listen to reason. When the calls kept coming from LaShawn, and then her attorney, Savon realized this crazy lie wouldn't go away without him taking action. But he hadn't contacted his attorney yet, because he didn't know if anyone would believe him, not even his legal team.

Savon took Bobbi's business card from his wallet. Maybe she could provide some professional advice. He had a clean slate with her, and she seemed trustworthy. Plus, it would give him an excuse to see her again. He placed the call.

"Good afternoon. My Way Communications, this is Ciara. How may I help you?"

"Hello . . . this is Savon Turner, calling for Miss Farqua."

"I'm sorry, Mister Turner," said the perky young assistant. "Miss Farqua is unavailable at the moment. Is there a message?"

"Sure." Savon left his number and a short message for Bobbi to return his call as soon as she could.

Ciara made a note of the information and ended the call. She went to Bobbi's office with the message from Savon and two other notes she'd taken that morning while Bobbi held a teleconference. She handed the slips of paper to Bobbi with Savon's message on top. Bobbi frowned when she saw his name.

"Oh, that message is from Mister Turner," said Ciara. "He just called and said it was urgent that he speak with you.

"Thanks, Ciara."

Bobbi skimmed over the other notes, and then took another look at the one from Savon. She couldn't imagine what urgent matter he needed to talk to her about. Bobbi had too much on her schedule today to get caught up in whatever Savon wanted. But she dialed his number anyway.

Savon answered and thanked Bobbi for returning his call, and then asked if he could meet with her in her office. He said that something important had come up and he wanted her professional advice. That piqued Bobbi's curiosity, but she didn't ask any questions. She checked her schedule and told him to come by between five and five-thirty.

Later that evening, Ciara froze in place when Savon walked into the office. She had been packing her things to leave for the day when he came through the door. Seeing athletes on TV didn't compare at all to laying eyes on them in person. She cleared her throat.

"May I help you?"

"Yes. I'm here to see Miss Farqua. I'm Savon Turner."

"Oh, yes. She's expecting you. Have a seat . . . she'll be right out." When Savon turned his back to walk to the sitting area, Ciara peered over the counter to get a better look. She fanned herself then buzzed Bobbi.

"Miss Farqua, Mister Turner is here to see you."

"Great. Can you bring him back? I'm on another call."

"Sure thing." Ciara hung up and escorted Savon to Bobbi's office.

Bobbi motioned for Savon to take a seat in front of her desk. She whispered thank you to Ciara and, seconds later, ended her call, giving Savon her complete focus.

"Hi, Savon. I'm almost afraid to ask how it's going."

"Yeah." Savon rubbed his head. "It's not too good."

"Before we get started, can I get you some water?" she said.

"Please."

Bobbi grabbed two bottles from the small refrigerator in the corner near the window, then handed Savon one. "So, tell me what's going on," she said, twisting the cap off hers.

Savon told Bobbi about LaShawn and the phone calls he'd been receiving for the last three weeks. He told her how the first call from LaShawn had been more of an invitation for the two of them to get reacquainted. But when he didn't take her up on the offer she'd flipped out and said he owed her back child support.

Savon let out a heavy sigh. "This woman is saying I'm the father of her two-year-old son."

"Well, are you?" Bobbi said matter-of-factly. She focused on Savon's body language and eye movement, looking for any indication of dishonesty.

"Absolutely not!" he said. "And now she's got her attorney calling and threatening me about child support."

"I have three questions for you Savon, so keep up. One and two: Did you have sex with her? And, if so, how can you be so sure it's not your child? And three: Why are you asking me for advice? I'm sure you have an attorney and a team of folks to help you."

"I tried to have sex with her, and I used protection. And yes, I have an attorney that I plan to call after I finish talking with you. But I wanted your opinion because I'm between publicists right now."

Bobbi didn't waste any time giving Savon her opinion. She told him that he should take everything LaShawn and her attorney said seriously, even if the child isn't his.

"Do you think she'll go public with this?" said Bobbi.

"Yeah, I think so. At least that's what she said last week, before her attorney called."

"Well, if that's true, I recommend you hire a publicist to represent you before the media gets hold of this. They love a good celebrity deadbeat dad story."

"Would you take me on as a client?" Savon held his breath. He didn't know how Bobbi felt about him as a client, but he liked the way she handled business. He even liked the way she handled him.

"You should call your attorney and bring him up to speed," she said. "After that, have him give me a call." Bobbi avoided his question. She didn't know if she wanted anything to do with Savon, let alone his paternity issue. And what in the heck did he mean by he "tried" to have sex with her? What kind of mess had Savon gotten himself into?

Chapter 7

Raymond Mayfield listened to Savon, wondering why he hadn't said anything until now. The stately man with salt and pepper hair had been Savon's attorney for the past five years. He'd rescued Savon from a few scorned women issues during that time, but this would be the most serious.

Once Savon finished telling him everything, Mayfield wanted to contact LaShawn's attorney before things got any worse. Savon's phone rang as Mayfield asked for the attorney's number.

"Hello," said Savon.

"Hey, have you seen the news?" said Bobbi.

"Nah, what's up?"

"You need to find a television or pull up CNN on your phone." Bobbi listened to the report on the TV in her office. "Your girl LaShawn chose today to go public with her story."

"What?!" Savon shook his head. *Monica.* He had hoped it wouldn't come to this—at least not until he had a chance to sit down with Monica and explain himself.

Bobbi was still on the line when Savon told Mayfield to follow him out to the television in the waiting area. Savon heard LaShawn's voice before he saw the television screen. She was on camera with the two-year-old boy and her attorney perpetrating a fraud.

"Savon Turner never bought my son not even one outfit," said LaShawn, frowning with disgust. "Never even gave him a drink of water. And I'm gonna make sure my son has everything he needs for the rest of his life."

Mayfield asked Savon for his phone to talk to Bobbi. Savon had told Mayfield about his visit to see Bobbi when he arrived at the office. Although it wasn't the ideal first meeting, if Bobbi had planned on being a part of Savon's case, the three of them needed to strategize.

Bobbi told Mayfield that she could be there in an hour and a half, and then Mayfield handed the phone back to Savon. But Bobbi had already hung up.

"So what do we do now?" said Savon.

"Bobbi agreed to meet us here in my office at eight-thirty," said Mayfield. He checked the time. "Maybe you should consider bringing Monica to the meeting. It may help her to see the support of your legal team. She'll hear the facts and know first-hand how we plan to handle things. Just a suggestion." Mayfield rested a reassuring hand on Savon's shoulder, and then left him standing there.

When Bobbi got off the phone with Mayfield, she slumped down in her seat. Savon had blind-sided her with his big bag of dirty laundry and expected her help. Asking her to work with his attorney to clear his name was a bit much. But how could she say no? In her office earlier and even over the phone a few minutes ago, he'd sounded so defeated.

After pulling together the necessary contractual documents, Bobbi locked up at My Way and headed over to the attorney's office. While driving, she prepared herself for the unknown as best she could. Managing crisis situations was her specialty, but the chance that Monica could be there had Bobbi on edge.

When she arrived at Mayfield's office, he'd already spoken to LaShawn's attorney. Mayfield told Bobbi and Savon that, based on the conversation, LaShawn wanted money—and lots of it. So their next move had to be a paternity test.

"Tell us the story, and don't leave anything out," said Mayfield, taking out his legal pad. "I need to understand why this woman is so adamant about you being the father."

Savon wiped his sweaty palms on his pants. Recounting the incident to them would help him build up the courage to tell Monica when he got home. So, he got up and paced the floor while Bobbi and Mayfield listened to the details of his encounter with LaShawn.

"It happened here in DC at an away game, when I played for the Atlanta Condors. After the game I went back to the hotel with the rest of the team and a few of us went downstairs to the bar to celebrate our win. That's when I met LaShawn. She was there with friends and we all hung out at the bar, drinking and talking trash. One thing led to the next and we ended up in my hotel room." Savon wrung his hands. "That vodka had me right, but I still strapped up. I know her son is not mine, because she passed out before I had a chance to get mine." Savon sat back down. "The whole scene kinda messed me up—I checked her pulse and everything. Then I left her on the bed and went to my boy's room. I never saw her again after that."

"Wow," said Bobbi. She found the story to be bizarre, far-fetched, and downright ridiculous. But then again, anything was possible with alcohol in the mix. And Savon seemed convinced that the boy wasn't his.

Mayfield made one last note on his pad and looked at Savon. "This mess will be over real soon. I'll order a paternity test for you and the boy—it will be as simple as that. Let's get you to the lab tomorrow."

"Okay. I hope so." Savon would do whatever it took to wake up from this nightmare.

Bobbi watched Savon while he talked with Mayfield. Something about that man turned her on. When he'd stopped by her office earlier, she'd been reminded of their magnetic chemistry. And she felt that same energy again right now. Bobbi cleared her throat to refocus on the matter at hand. "Savon. Why don't you come over here and look over this contract?" She patted the seat next to her.

Attorney Mayfield excused himself while they handled business. Bobbi explained the services she offered for this particular situation and provided ideas for supporting his career and brand long term. While she waited for Savon to flip through the pages, she took the opportunity to draft a statement for immediate release. The media had already contacted him for comment so, once she had his signature, Bobbi would make a statement on his behalf and send out a press release. At this point, a personal appearance was premature. They would hold off on an actual press conference until they had the paternity test results.

Savon looked at Bobbi. "I'm ready to sign."

Bobbi handed him a pen. "So, are you a temporary client or does My Way have your business for the foreseeable future?"

"You couldn't get rid of me if you wanted to," he said.

Bobbi bumped his arm with hers and smiled. "Check this out." She handed him a draft of the statement she planned to send out tonight.

Mr. Turner has requested a paternity test and is confident this misunderstanding will be resolved shortly. He asks that the media respect his privacy until the results are back. Thank you.

"That's what's up," said Savon. "You're sending it tonight?"
"Yep. Soon as you sign the papers."

———⊳●⊲———

"So you finally decided to come home, huh?" said Monica, standing in the doorway.

"I told you I had to meet with my attorney and publicist. If you didn't trust me, you should have come." Savon brushed past Monica and tossed his keys in the glass bowl on the table in the foyer.

"Trust? What the heck could you possibly know about trust, huh? Here I am walking around on your arm, wearing your ring, and you're out there sleeping around and making babies. Don't talk to me about trust." Monica followed Savon to the family room.

"Look, Monica," Savon plopped down on the sofa, "I'm sorry this happened. But I told you it's not my kid. Why can't you try to understand and support me on this?"

Monica stood in front of Savon, staring down at him. "You have some hood-rat and her child on TV saying you're the father, and you want me to understand? Hah!" She bent down in his face, her eyes like slits. "You're pathetic and you don't deserve me. I'm outta here." Monica stormed off toward the staircase.

Savon jumped up off the sofa and went after her. He grabbed her arm before she made it to the first step.

"All that happened three years ago," he said. "You and I were just dating at the time, so why are you trippin'?"

"Whatever. Have fun with your hood-rat." Monica snatched her arm away and went upstairs to finish packing her bags. Within an hour, she was out the door.

Bobbi was exhausted by the time she got home. She took a hot shower and put on her favorite red silk robe from Korea with the embossed dragon on the back—one of her cherished mementos from the military.

In the kitchen, she fixed a salad and then went to watch television in the family room. Afterwards, she looked over some papers from work and checked her phone messages. As expected, she had a call from Nikki, asking if she'd heard about Savon. There were also messages from Tony and her mom.

She returned her mom's call first, since Grace went to bed early. Bobbi still hadn't told her about meeting Lance. She'd prayed every day not to bump into him again, since the night he changed her flat.

Next she called Tony. They hadn't seen each other in a while, but that didn't mean anything. He answered and they teased each other until they were both hot and bothered. Then they scheduled a midnight rendezvous for Friday night.

When Bobbi called Nikki, she picked up after the first ring.

"Give it up, Miss PR. I know you have the 4-1-1 on ya boy," Nikki prodded.

"Oh, I'm fine. Thanks for asking. How are you?" said Bobbi.

Nikki smacked her lips. "I don't have time for pleasantries. What I want to know is what's up with Savon and I know you know something."

"And you would be right," said Bobbi. "As of nine o'clock this evening, Savon is officially a client at My Way. Woot Woot!"

"Seriously?" Nikki's jaw dropped. "How'd that happen?"

Bobbi recounted the story, starting with Savon's call to her office that afternoon. She gave Nikki the details about LaShawn but stopped short of telling her what Savon had revealed in Mayfield's office. That would remain in her confidence.

Chapter 8

Bobbi stood in a restaurant parking lot talking to Savon after meeting him for dinner. Now that she was his publicist, he came up with reasons for them to meet and talk about business even after work hours. Just like tonight.

"Thanks for believing in me," he said, stepping closer to her. "I need someone in my corner right now."

"Of course," said Bobbi. She could smell the red wine on his breath. "I appreciate your honesty and being real about what happened. It makes what I do worthwhile."

Savon looked into her eyes and closed the small space between them and embraced her. Dang, he smelled good—crisp and masculine. Her immediate thought had been to say something silly to lighten the mood, but he kissed her on the forehead and then released her.

"Thanks, again . . . for everything," he said and opened her car door.

"You're welcome."

Bobbi got in and pulled off. In the rearview mirror, she saw him standing there next to his chromed out, black Escalade, watching her disappear into the night.

A week later, Bobbi sat on the sofa in her office with her shoes off, playing a puzzle app on her smartphone. Ciara buzzed in to let her know that Savon was there, and she told her to send him back.

"What's going on?" said Bobbi when he entered the office.

"Hey there . . . not much. Just stopped by to see what you're up to."

Before Savon had invaded her space the other night in the parking lot with that forehead kiss, she actually didn't mind his visits. She'd blocked out time on her schedule to meet with him a couple days a week and really enjoyed his company. But now she needed to be on guard.

Savon sat down across from Bobbi and right away, he started talking about Monica. This wasn't Bobbi's favorite topic of course, but she felt sorry for the man and wanted to be supportive. So she let him get whatever he needed to off his chest.

He spent twenty minutes telling her that he'd been overwhelmed with all the troubles in his life. Monica wouldn't respond to his calls. LaShawn hadn't taken her son for DNA testing. He had to deal with rumors and the questioning stares of his coaches and teammates. And to top it off, the media wouldn't stop bugging him.

Bobbi changed the subject when he took a breath after his comment about the media. She'd had enough of his saga and wanted to talk business. Bobbi told Savon that she had a meeting scheduled with Under Amour next week for an endorsement deal and he looked up toward the ceiling, shaking his head.

"Are you serious? I've always wanted to work with them."

"We're almost there. I'm closing this deal next week." She winked at him.

Bobbi went over to her desk to give Savon more details about the deal and he hugged her when she stepped by him. They laughed at the gesture and then chatted more about endorsements and football season before Bobbi walked him out.

When they made it to Ciara's desk, Bobbi's head jerked back and she forced a smile when she saw Lance sitting in the waiting area.

"Hi, Lance. Give me a minute."

Lance got up and nodded his acknowledgment.

Savon looked at Lance and then back at Bobbi—his eyebrow raised. Bobbi noticed but ignored it. Savon wasn't her man, and neither was Lance for that matter. She told Savon good-bye, grinning on the inside at his reaction. He even tried to spark a conversation with Ciara to stick around a little longer. But when Bobbi turned toward Lance, Savon stuck out his chest and walked out of the suite.

Now what? Bobbi hadn't expected Lance to come find her. In her attempt to not mislead him, she'd mishandled things, which made seeing him right now so awkward. She owed Lance an apology. And once she learned the reason for his visit, she would do just that.

"Hey," said Bobbi, "this is a surprise. You found me."

Lance chuckled. "I did."

"Well, come on back to my office."

Bobbi led the way, wondering why Ciara didn't let her know that Lance had been waiting to see her. She cut her eye at Ciara. They would talk about this little mishap later.

Lance admired Bobbi's feminine office décor as he took a seat on the sofa.

"I wanted to stop by and check on you," he said. "I know you're a busy lady, so I won't hold you. I just wanted to say hello."

Bobbi swallowed hard. See. This is what she'd been concerned about. She didn't want him to be sensitive toward her, checking in to see if things were okay and expecting her to be sweet and accommodating.

"Aw, that's so kind of you," she said. "I should have called to let you know I made it home that night. Please forgive my bad manners. I really do appreciate what you did—and I cringe at the thought of how things could've turned out if you weren't there."

"No need to apologize. I just wanted to make sure you were okay." Lance stood to leave. "Now that I see you're alive and well, I'll let you get back to work."

Bobbi smiled. "Well, I'm glad you stopped by. Don't be a stranger." What else could she say?

Lance touched her arm and said, "I'll show myself out."

Chapter 9

Finally, the DNA results were back. Attorney Mayfield had called on a few favors to push things through and the good news came in on Labor Day.

"Yes!" Bobbi shouted into the phone. "Whew. I didn't doubt Savon, but it's good to hear that he's in the clear." She did a dance. "Can I give him the news?"

"Sure," said Mayfield. "But make sure you tell Savon to call me so we can move forward with our defense. The three of us can meet tomorrow to get the ball rolling."

"Will do. I'm on my way after we hang up."

Bobbi got dressed, put her hair in a bun and left. Halfway to Savon's house, she called to make sure he was home. Although she'd never been to his house before, she knew where he lived. When he answered, she asked if she could stop by to discuss something concerning the case, and he hesitated. Bobbi laughed at his attempt to find the words to respond, and then assured him that it wouldn't take long.

Fifteen minutes later, she parked in his circular driveway and made her way to the front door and rang the bell. Her cheeks hurt, she smiled so hard.

"This is a nice surprise?" said Savon when he opened the door.

Bobbi didn't know whether to melt or talk. "I have something to tell you," she sang.

"What?" He stepped aside and let her in.

Bobbi followed him, but she didn't take a seat when he offered. Instead, she told him that she needed to stand for what she had to say. For a brief moment, she just stared at him, smiling.

"In the words of Maury Povich: Savon Turner, you are 'not' the father."

It took a few seconds for Bobbi's words to register. "Are you serious?" he said, both hands on his head. "It's finally over? Four weeks of hell. It's finally over!"

Caught up in the moment, Savon lifted Bobbi off the floor, spinning her around in circles. They both laughed. When the reality of their closeness hit, Savon stopped in his tracks. Bobbi was still in his arms, her feet dangling at least a foot above the floor. Their eyes locked.

"Uhhh . . . you can put me down now," she said.

Savon didn't say a word. His grip loosened just enough for her body to slide slowly down the length of his. He bent down to kiss her and she threw her arms around his neck to pull him closer.

Savon's ringing telephone interrupted them, and they released each other.

Bobbi hoped he would, but realized he wasn't going to answer the phone by the third ring. She glanced up at him and his eyes were glazed over. Bobbi looked away, brushing imaginary lint from her shirt.

She cleared her throat. "Uhh . . . I think I should go."

He brushed his index finger across her cheek. "Okay." He walked her to the door.

Bobbi took a deep breath to regain her composure. "I almost forgot. Mayfield wants you to call him right away. He also said the three of us need to meet tomorrow." She looked at him with genuine sincerity. "Congratulations, Savon."

"Thanks for coming by to give me the news," he said.

Bobbi waved good-bye and got out of there. She hoped she didn't look like a lunatic—and she hoped Savon couldn't tell how much she'd been shaken by his kiss.

Bobbi was beside herself as she drove out of Savon's neighborhood. How could she let this happen? Kissing him felt so right, yet it was wrong on so many levels.

Stopped at a red light, that life-altering kiss played tricks with her mind. Her heart raced and her body tingled. She tried to shake the feeling, but she couldn't. She wanted Savon.

When the light turned green, Bobbi silenced her thoughts and all the reasons why she shouldn't sleep with him. A window of opportunity had presented itself and she couldn't let it pass her by. She swung a U-turn and went back.

Savon opened the door and winked at her. He reached for her hand and pulled her inside. She started to say something, but he shook his head, putting a finger to her lips. Then he kissed her.

He took Bobbi upstairs to his bedroom, where they spent the rest of the day. Every part of her body received preferential treatment. If she tried to take control, he would shake his head and give her more pleasure. He only stopped long enough to feed her, and back to it they went. At times, if she didn't know better, she could've sworn they'd made love.

At midnight, Bobbi pulled into her driveway. She headed straight for the kitchen to try and replenish what she'd lost in the throes of passion. Her sodium level had to be dangerously low. She grinned. Savon was a gifted man. They had done things to each other she was embarrassed to remember, let alone talk about. A chill went up her spine and her shoulders shimmied at the thought.

All jokes aside, Bobbi had to remind herself that they'd had sex, nothing more. She popped a strawberry in her mouth and carried a plate of cheese and crackers to her room. After finishing the snack, Bobbi lay across the bed thinking about the last thirteen hours. What now?

The next morning, Bobbi met Savon at attorney Mayfield's office. When they saw each other, he didn't act weird, which helped Bobbi to relax. She had been anxious about seeing him today. But thank goodness Savon had proven that he could be mature enough to blur the lines with business and personal, and still be normal.

Mayfield, Bobbi, and Savon agreed that the time had come for a press conference. They wanted to make it known that Savon's only crime had been choosing the wrong woman to sleep with. So Bobbi arranged a meeting with the press for two o'clock that same day.

They drove separate cars to the press conference location. Bobbi arrived early to make sure there would be no surprises for her client. Then Savon and Mayfield showed up around one forty-five. At two o'clock, Mayfield stepped up to the mic with Savon standing behind him and Bobbi at his side.

"Savon Turner is not the biological father of LaShawn Dawson's son," said Mayfield. "The paternity results are conclusive."

After the announcement, Savon stepped up to the podium to answer a few questions with Bobbi close by. A reporter asked what really happened and Savon took the high road, saying that all he cared about was moving forward with his life and the football season.

When the press conference ended, Bobbi went back to her office. It was five o'clock and Ciara had gone for the day. Bobbi checked her messages and looked over her schedule for the rest of the week. She rubbed the back of her neck. What a taxing day. Pushing her laptop aside, she rested her head on the desk. Fifteen minutes later, the phone rang, waking her.

"Hello." Bobbi wiped drool from the corner of her mouth.

"What are you doing?" said Savon.

"About to leave work. What's up?"

"Can I take you to dinner to celebrate?" he said.

"Uh . . . I'm a little tired tonight. Can I take a rain check?" Bobbi thought maybe she'd had enough of Mister Wonderful for one day.

"Come on, I really want to show my appreciation. After tonight, I'll be on the road for the next two weeks. You can rest after I leave." The line was quiet, so Savon added, "Don't make me beg, because I will if I have to."

"Hmmm. I might like that," said Bobbi. "What would you say?"

Savon played along. "My feelings would be hurt if you didn't accept my invitation. You have believed in me since day one. So, please, do me the honor of celebrating our victory with me tonight."

Bobbi applauded. "That was pretty good, Mister Turner." She shifted in her seat. "How can I turn down an invitation like that?"

Later that night, Bobbi sat at the kitchen table checking her social media accounts while she waited for Savon to get there. When he arrived, she went to answer the door.

"Nice—very nice," he said, admiring the sexy vixen in the little black dress that stood before him.

"Thank you. I'm ready." Bobbi loved the reaction she inspired in Savon. She grabbed her things off the table and joined him.

He opened the door to his Escalade and she climbed in and got comfortable, watching as he walked around the front of the SUV. Savon had to be the finest man in America.

Before he pulled off, Savon asked Bobbi if she had a music preference and she said no. Although it had been sweet of him to ask, it didn't matter. Right now, Bobbi's thoughts were stuck on him and what had happened between them yesterday. One thing she knew for sure—she wasn't done with him yet.

Savon had reservations at an exclusive DC restaurant. Even with his clout, Bobbi wondered how he'd managed to pull it off in a matter of hours.

While they waited to be seated, Savon's hand rested on the small of her back. She didn't know how many more of his displays of intimacy she could take without reciprocating. Whether he knew it or not, he'd been testing her respect for his engagement. If he didn't start behaving like a man with a fiancée, she couldn't be held responsible for her actions.

The hostess escorted them to a table in a corner near a grand piano. Savon pulled out her chair and then took his. The server brought a wine list and menus, recommending a white Merlot to start the evening.

Bobbi looked around the restaurant while Savon talked to the server. This didn't feel like a celebratory dinner with a client at all. Everything about Savon tonight—from the way he looked at her to the way he handled her to the tone of his voice—made it clear that they were on a date.

During dinner, Savon asked Bobbi to taste his prime rib, and then he fed her. She played along and did the same with her grilled swordfish. Bobbi made a toast to his name being cleared and Savon reached for her free hand and squeezed it.

By the time they finished dinner and pulled into her driveway, it was eleven-thirty. They both had to get up early the next morning, but neither wanted the night to end. So Bobbi invited him inside.

"Can I get you something to drink?" she said, taking off her jacket.

"Water."

Savon's jaw clenched. Their closeness tonight made him crazy. He couldn't dismiss the bulge in his pants any longer. When Bobbi returned, he took the glass from her hand. "Sit with me," he said. Then he whispered in her ear, "I want you."

Her body responded to his demand like he owned it. The little black dress came undone and so did she as he made love to her right there on the sectional sofa.

The next morning, Bobbi sat at her desk, processing the whirlwind of events that had taken place over the last forty-eight hours. She sipped her latte. Savon was her client and her lover, but another woman wore his ring. Bobbi sighed. Why did she like him so much?

Scrolling through her email, Bobbi remembered that she hadn't returned Nikki's call from yesterday. Nikki had left a message inquiring about Savon after seeing the press conference. Bobbi made the call.

"Well dang," said Nikki. "Good thing a sistah wasn't in jail or needed a ride to the ER or something. I called you like three days ago."

"You called me yesterday, drama queen." Bobbi laughed.

"Whatever. So, Savon is not the father, huh?"

"Nope. He was telling the truth," said Bobbi.

"Another groupie bites the dust." Nikki digressed. "So . . . what's been up with you?"

"Ahh . . . what are you doing this weekend?" said Bobbi, dismissing Nikki's question. Bobbi wanted to tell Nikki that she'd been sleeping with Savon, but she preferred to drop that bomb in person.

"I'm working. Why . . . what's up?" said Nikki.

"I need to talk to you about something. What about next weekend?"

"I'm going home—remember? Mom is catering a wedding next Saturday and she needs help."

"Maybe I'll go with you," said Bobbi.

"You should. Mom would love that," Nikki replied.

Chapter 10

Two weeks later, Nikki and Bobbi arrived in Atlanta. They talked nonstop on the plane, but Bobbi still hadn't mentioned that she'd slept with Savon.

Nikki signed for the rental car and they took a detour to check out the summer clearance racks at the mall instead of going straight home. It had been Bobbi's idea to do so since she still hadn't found just the right words to share her little secret with Nikki. But she couldn't stall any longer. She would get it out at the mall before they got caught up in family matters later that evening.

Walking through the food court, a woman at the Chinese food counter called them over to sample some chicken on a toothpick. Neither had eaten, so Bobbi figured what better time than over a meal to tell Nikki what she'd been up to.

Bobbi got her tray first and headed for a table in the center of the food court, away from the other patrons. Nikki could be a bit dramatic and Bobbi hoped to keep her embarrassment to a minimum. When they started eating, Bobbi dropped the bomb.

"I slept with Savon."

Nikki choked on her rice, but still managed to get out, "Say what? Please tell me you didn't." She wiped her mouth. "When?"

"Two weeks ago, when I went to his house to give him the DNA news." Bobbi shrugged her shoulders. "I mean . . . one thing led to the next, and his tongue was down my throat."

"First of all, I don't understand how your client's tongue ended up in your mouth. But you slept with him? Dang, B." Nikki didn't hide her disappointment. Bobbi deserved more than what Savon had to offer.

Bobbi talked about Savon and what they'd been up to, including some details about their sexual encounters. But judging from the frown lines forming around her nose, it was clear that Nikki didn't like the news one bit. Bobbi knew that Nikki didn't want to hear her go on about this man, but whom else could she tell? She'd darn near burst trying to hold it in these last two weeks.

When Nikki asked about Savon's fiancée, Bobbi couldn't answer because she didn't know their status. She never asked and she didn't care. Nothing about Monica interested her.

The friends finished lunch and strolled through the mall. In the Nordstrom shoe department, they browsed the clearance racks and tried on a few pairs before deciding which ones to purchase. Then they moved on to the MAC make-up counter where they both picked up a new fall shade.

After swiping her card and signing the receipt, Bobbi didn't look up as she put her credit card back in her wallet. Two steps in, she collided with another shopper.

"Oops—excuse me," said Bobbi.

Monica's lips formed to say excuse me too until she realized who she'd bumped into.

"You're Monica, right?" said Bobbi. "We met in DC over the summer." Bobbi tried to downplay her surprise. What were the chances of running into Monica in Atlanta?

Monica rolled her eyes, giving her two friends a girl-please look.

Bobbi glanced at Nikki, who then reached up and unhooked her hoop earrings, dropping them in her purse. Bobbi grinned. She knew her girl had her back, even if she didn't approve of her dealings with Savon.

Seconds felt like minutes as they had a standoff. Bobbi smirked. She wanted to tell Monica that she'd been taking real good care of Savon. But now wasn't the time or place. The opportunity to share her thoughts with Monica would come again. It was inevitable, especially if she kept seeing Savon.

Monica flicked her hair over her shoulder and she and her goons walked off like they had won a battle. Then Nikki grabbed Bobbi by the arm and led her in the opposite direction, back into the mall.

"I have one question," said Nikki. "Are you done with Savon?"

"What do you mean?" said Bobbi.

"Seriously? That girl, Monica, is loco. I thought I was gonna have to fight just now. She's bound to find out about you and Savon. Then what?"

"Do I look like I care?" Bobbi bucked her eyes. "Her game is busted . . . and Savon is the one pursuing me, not the other way around. So, if she finds out and wants to address it—then we'll see what's up."

"This is crazy, B." Nikki shook her head. "That Savon must be a stallion." Nikki laughed and threw her arm around Bobbi's shoulder as they walked back toward the food court and out of the mall.

Tony called to see if Bobbi wanted to do dinner and a movie and she jumped at the chance to do something to distract her from thinking about Savon. Who by the way, she hadn't heard from since the night they celebrated him being cleared of paternity, three weeks ago.

When Bobbi arrived at Tony's house, he greeted her with a small kiss. She followed him into the kitchen and he asked her to check show times for the movie while he went upstairs to get his wallet. She sat in front of his laptop and narrowed down her choices, and when he returned, he purchased the tickets online and they headed out.

Later for dinner, they went to a quaint bistro with a live jazz band. It was one of their favorite spots. They ordered dinner and talked about the movie, and then Tony asked about Savon. Bobbi had hoped it wouldn't come up, but Tony wanted to know about the paternity debacle. She realized that all of her friends knew she represented him now, thanks to the press conference. However, the point of being out with Tony tonight had been to get Savon out of her head.

Bobbi pointed at a man doing old school dances in the area next to the band. Tony turned to look and they both laughed. She'd been tapping her feet and swaying side-to-side since they'd sat down, so she understood why the man couldn't keep his seat. When the music slowed down and Bobbi heard the first bar of a familiar ballad, she asked Tony to dance.

On the floor, he pulled her close and they moved in sync to the sultry sound of the saxophone. When they returned to the table, the server had just arrived with their dinner plates. After eating, they danced a while longer and then left.

On the short ride back to Tony's house, Bobbi hummed along to the jazz tune playing on the radio. The night had been wonderful. She and Tony never had any drama. Their romance allowed her to be easy and carefree—that's what she needed.

When they got to his house, Tony opened the car door and reached for her hand, holding it as they went inside. Bobbi knew he wasn't ready for her to leave, and neither was she.

"I've waited all night for this," said Tony, undressing her.

Bobbi wrapped her arms around his neck when he leaned down to kiss her. He pulled back the covers and laid her down in his bed. He satisfied her first and then himself, ending their evening on a high note.

As Tony slept, the rise and fall of his chest made for a peaceful backdrop to Bobbi's thoughts of Savon. Why did she care about him? He could give two flying flips about her or he would have called by now. Bobbi turned to look at the clock on the dresser. It was one-thirty. She rolled out of Tony's arms and got dressed.

She patted Tony's shoulder. "Walk me out."

"You don't have to leave. It's too late—" His words trailed off.

Bobbi shook him. "Wake up. I know it's late, but I want to go home." She smacked his butt. "Come on . . . get up."

"Okay, okay."

A drowsy Tony fumbled around for his pants and walked Bobbi out to her car. He opened her door and then hugged her. "Call me when you get home."

"Alright, sleepy head."

Bobbi cranked up the music to help her stay awake on the thirty-minute drive home. She was throwing her hands in the air and rapping when her phone rang. The Bluetooth picked up the signal from the phone, and her heart skipped a beat.

At the third ring, Bobbi still contemplated whether she should answer. It had been darn near a month since she'd heard from Savon. She gritted her teeth, reminding herself that he was a client, and picked up.

"Hello." Bobbi blurted. He had some nerve to go without calling her. Humph.

"What's up, Bobbi? How are you?" he said.

"Hi, stranger. I'm well. You do realize it's almost two in the morning, right?"

Savon cleared his throat. "I need to talk to you. Can I come over?"

"Come over? What's going on?" Bobbi switched into publicist mode.

He sighed. "Monica's trippin'. She said she saw you in Atlanta last weekend, and then asked me if I was sleeping with you. Did you say something to her?"

"Hold up." Bobbi sat up taller in her seat. "I don't know where you're going with this—so let me help you. I ran into her at the mall and she was just as ignorant then as she was the first time I met her. I spoke and she didn't, and that was it."

"Okay, Bobbi." He spoke slowly. "But I still want to talk to you, though. Can I come over?"

"I'm not home. We can meet for lunch tomorrow." He had balls the size of eggplants to think she would entertain him tonight.

"Okay," Savon conceded.

Bobbi ended the call as she pulled into her garage. She called Tony and he mumbled into the phone. She chuckled, thinking he probably wouldn't even remember that she called.

Bobbi said her prayers and got in bed. She couldn't believe Savon had asked if she'd told Monica they were sleeping together. He didn't have the sense of a goat. Why would he even ask her that? Bobbi didn't care if they ever hung out again. Tomorrow she would give him the opportunity to speak his mind, and that would be it. From then on, their relationship would be business and nothing more. Bobbi pulled the covers over her head. Savon's problems with Monica were not hers, and she refused to get caught up in their madness.

Chapter 11

After running errands, Bobbi met Savon for lunch. When she pulled into the parking lot, she saw him standing at the entrance to the restaurant looking down at his smartphone. She parked, prayed for patience and then went to join him.

"Wow . . . you look nice," he said, giving her a small peck on the cheek. He got a whiff of that warm, citrusy fragrance he liked so much.

"Hey you," she said.

A freckle-faced hostess seated them at a table and left.

Bobbi could feel Savon's eyes on her. "Did you ask me here to stare at me, or are we here to talk?" she said, looking up from the menu.

"I'm not staring at you." Savon chuckled. "You changed your hair. I like it."

"Thanks." Bobbi put the menu down. "So what's up, for real?" she said.

Savon shifted in his seat. He proceeded to tell Bobbi that Monica hadn't returned any of his calls except to say that she needed her space and time to think about their relationship. Then out of nowhere, she had called and asked if he was sleeping with her.

Bobbi pretended to listen, trying not to yawn and roll her eyes. She had checked out on his monologue, one minute in. He could not be serious right now. In case he didn't remember, they had in fact done a lot more than just sleep together. But he'd made it clear that what they shared didn't rate higher than what he wanted with Monica. So she would accept that and move on. They were both stupid anyways.

Savon finished his dumb story by saying that Monica was on her way back to DC in a couple of days to try and reconcile their differences. The nerve of this joker!

"Well, dang," said Bobbi. "That sure was a mouthful. But you do remember that we did actually sleep together, right?"

"Uhm . . . yeah. But I'm saying, that's our business . . . nobody else's."

"Not anymore, it isn't," said Bobbi, trying not to raise her voice. "You and me, and whatever we were doing, is over."

The wrinkles in Savon's forehead deepened. "What do you mean?"

Bobbi looked at her salad and pushed it away. She had to enlighten this fool. "Listen, Savon. I call the shots in my life. You and I had our fling or whatever you wanna call it because I decided that's what I wanted. You and Monica can do whatever you need to do, just keep me out of it. I don't need to know all of this." She pushed back in her chair. "Oh . . . and don't worry, business is still business." She extended her hand. "Friends?"

"Uhm . . . yeah. Friends," he said, shaking her hand. Savon wasn't sure what the heck had just happened. He had wanted to make sure Bobbi wasn't expecting anything from him, especially with Monica coming back. But somehow, he'd lost control of the conversation.

When Bobbi got in the car, she screamed. Savon had some nerve to think he could sleep with her and then expect her to act like it never happened—all for Monica's sake? Ooh! If she weren't a dignified, God-fearing, scared-of-the-law businesswoman, all four rims on that Escalade would be kissing the pavement.

Bobbi cranked up and pulled off. She needed to sever the business side of things, and soon. But she couldn't do it right now while her feelings ran deep or else she'd come off like the proverbial woman scorned. Figuring out the timing to drop Savon from the roster at My Way would be her first priority starting today.

Later that night, Bobbi sat in her living room listening to a message from her mother. As usual, Grace had asked about Lance. After deleting the recording, Bobbi pulled up Lance's number in her phone. He'd helped her out and had even stopped by her office to check on her. Getting to know someone like that couldn't be a bad thing. Plus, she needed to come clean with him.

Bobbi shook off the nervous energy and placed the call.

"I was just about to hang up, Mister Holder. How are you? It's Bobbi."

Lance laughed. "I'm glad you didn't. I was chasing after my daughter—she took my phone and ran when it started ringing. Hold on a minute," said Lance. His daughter was calling for him in the background.

Bobbi held the line. She could hear the cuteness in his daughter's tiny voice calling for daddy, but she knew his reality wasn't for her. Lance could grow to be a good friend and maybe even a potential client. But for now, Bobbi would clear the air—and her conscience—and they could get to know each other if he wanted to.

"I'm back," said Lance.

"What's your daughter's name?"

"Ava."

"Lance. I see you're busy with Ava, so I won't hold you. But I wanted to confirm what I'm sure you already know. I'm Grace's daughter." She grinned. "After you gave me your business card, I realized you were the same person she'd been telling me about. So I was a little bit embarrassed to call after you were so kind to help me. And I apologize for not—"

Lance cut her off.

"That's enough," he said. "I get it. And I appreciate you telling me what the deal was. But I understand people are busy. Your mother is a sweet lady, so I know the apple didn't fall far from the tree." Lance chuckled. "It's all good."

"Thanks for understanding."

"No worries."

"Well, alright then. I'll let you get back to Ava. Don't be a stranger," said Bobbi.

"Never," said Lance.

———※※———

The following weekend, Bobbi, Gavin, Nikki, and Nikki's boo, Todd, all met at Indi Red to celebrate Bobbi's birthday. Bobbi wasn't in the mood to make a fuss over her big day, but Nikki had insisted on getting together with a few friends for dinner and drinks. And now Bobbi was glad she'd agreed.

She hadn't realized how much she needed this outing. So much of her time had to be devoted to pleasing people and stroking egos that she often overlooked moments to celebrate her own life—but not tonight.

During dinner, the group talked about current events, sports, and the latest gossip around town. Then Nikki and Todd started whispering to each other, forgetting that Bobbi and Gavin were even there.

"Is everything okay?" asked the waiter while clearing away their appetizer dishes.

"We need another bottle of champagne," said Gavin, receiving nods of approval from around the table.

Nikki and Bobbi were talking when the server returned with the bubbly, and Gavin interrupted them to make a toast. He filled their glasses and they all lifted them toward the center of the table.

"Here's to you, Bobbi—the finest girl at this table. Turn up!" Gavin threw his arm around her shoulder and kissed her cheek.

They all laughed as their glasses clinked.

"Thanks, sweetie," said Bobbi.

"The finest girl at the table, huh?" said Nikki. "So what am I . . . pulled pork?"

Gavin waved off Nikki's comment and pulled Bobbi closer to him.

Across the restaurant, Savon sat at a table with Monica. From the time the hostess had seated them an hour ago, his eyes were on Bobbi and her friends. He wondered why Gavin's hands had been on some part of Bobbi the whole time. And he also wanted to know why Gavin had just kissed her face.

He and Gavin weren't the best of friends, but as teammates they respected each other. They had even hung out after a few games. That's how he knew Gavin and Nikki were blood cousins, and that he considered Bobbi to be family.

Savon wanted to go over and speak, but he didn't know how Bobbi would respond, considering how they clashed the last time they met up. Plus, Savon couldn't risk Monica seeing Bobbi and causing a fight. So far, she hadn't noticed Bobbi, and if he could help it, she never would. He didn't want to argue tonight.

Monica had just come back to DC three days ago, and it had taken him until tonight to calm her down enough for them to enjoy a peaceful night out on the town. So, not even Bobbi with her fine self would be worth disturbing this moment of unity. However, he had to find a reason to call Bobbi—and soon.

Chapter 12

The Warriors were fighting for their spot in the play-offs, and Savon found himself working just as hard at home to hold things together. He and Monica were in the same house, sleeping in the same bed, but she wouldn't let him touch her. Instead of pleasing her man, she had been obsessed with hating Bobbi. If she only knew—a little action a few days a week might keep a lid on his desire for Bobbi.

Nonetheless, even though things were rocky between them, Savon tried hard to make it work. For example, tonight they were on their way to a charity dinner for his best friend's foundation. This outing would be one of many things he wanted to do to prove to Monica that he could be a trusted and loving fiancé.

"Are you ready?" said Monica.

"Yeah," said Savon, standing in the mirror fixing his tie.

Monica stepped in front of him and took over. "Here," she said. "Let me do that."

Savon watched Monica tie his tie, and tried to remember where things had gone wrong for them. She'd been hostile for a long time, and he couldn't for the life of him pinpoint when it had started.

"There," she said, folding down his collar over the tie.

Savon looked in the mirror and wiggled the knot. "Okay. That's good. Let's go." He grabbed his keys off the dresser and they left.

When they arrived at the W-Hotel, Savon handed the keys to the valet attendant and they went inside. He found their table and made sure Monica was seated and didn't need anything before going over to greet his homeboy.

"What's up, Derek?" said Savon. "Nice turn out."

"What up, man?" Derek said. "Yeah, my publicist got the word out."

"It's a good cause."

Savon and Derek talked a while longer, and Derek introduced him to some other folks that worked for the foundation. Then Savon looked across the room, wondering what Monica was up to.

"I'll holla at you later, man," said Savon. "Let me get back to my lady."

"Okay . . . bet."

After speaking to a number of other acquaintances, Savon went back to his table where he found Monica conversing with another couple. She seemed to be enjoying herself for a change. Seeing her smile and even laugh, helped Savon to relax. He crossed his fingers. Maybe he would get some tonight.

The moderator for the event asked for people to be seated, and then introduced Derek, who welcomed and thanked everyone for coming. Savon reached for Monica's hand under the table and she blushed as their fingers touched. This was a small thing, but a huge step in getting them back to a good place. Savon leaned over and kissed her and she smiled.

During the meal, Monica made small talk about the event and how nice it had been for them to dress in formal attire and do something different. Fancy restaurants and dining out was the popular thing to do in DC, but Monica found it to be overrated. They saw the same people all the time everywhere they went.

"Uhm," said Monica, taking the napkin from her lap and dabbing at her lips. "I wanted to apologize for my behavior lately. You don't deserve it, and I promise to do better."

"Say that again." Savon took out his iPhone. "I want to record you, just in case you forget what you said."

She swatted at him and they both laughed. Then Savon pulled her closer.

When the keynote speaker finished, the moderator announced a fifteen-minute break before the auction started. Monica went to the restroom, but not before sharing a kiss with her man. Savon smiled as she walked away—fantasizing about how good the make-up sex would be tonight.

Monica returned to the table and Savon stood up to pull out her chair. Before he took his seat, he saw Bobbi walking to a table on the other side of the room. He let out a deep breath. That woman was his fantasy, manifested. The winter white gown she wore, fit like a glove. Sweat beads formed on his forehead and he wiped them away with a handkerchief he pulled from his coat pocket.

Savon missed Bobbi—and so did his manhood. He'd initiated a number of business calls over the last few weeks hoping to strike up some personal dialogue, but she'd kept things professional. Nothing in her voice had indicated that she missed him too.

He watched Bobbi sit down next to a guy, who put his arm around her shoulders, and then leaned in to say something in her ear. She laughed and pecked his lips. Savon didn't know what to do. His stomach turned. Should he go over and say something?

Savon couldn't believe how comfortable they seemed with each other. In all the time he'd spent with Bobbi, she never mentioned seeing someone else.

Monica frowned at Savon. "Something wrong?"

"Nah . . . I'm good," he said with a nervous grin, taking off his dinner jacket. The last thing he wanted to do was draw attention to Bobbi sitting a hundred feet away.

But Savon couldn't keep his attention focused on his own table, and before long, Monica followed his stare across the room to find Bobbi looking back at her.

"Really, Savon?" she said. Her body started to trembled. "Take me home. Right now!" Monica got up and threw a glass of wine in his face and stormed off.

Embarrassed, Savon rubbed a hand over his face and brushed the liquid from his shirt. The couple that Monica had befriended asked if he was okay and he nodded. Others at the table and those sitting close enough to see and hear what had happened were staring and whispering. Savon put back on his jacket, glanced over at Bobbi, and then went after Monica.

He found her standing outside waiting for the Escalade. So, he went to stand next to her and saw tear stains on her face. She ignored him and he dropped his head, regretting that he'd hurt her again. When the valet pulled up, he paid the fee while Monica snatched open the passenger side door, breaking a nail. Savon climbed in and pulled off without a word. Noise from the radio filled the awkward space between them until Monica turned it off and faced him.

"I get it now," she said. "You don't want to get married—you never did. You just want to hang on to me while you strut around DC, sleeping with every slut you meet!" She wanted to claw his eyeballs out. "Why . . . why am I here?"

Savon kept his eyes on the road, looking straight ahead like a robot. He didn't say a word, which enraged Monica even more.

"You don't have anything to say?" She waited. "You are so disrespectful—so disrespectful." Monica wanted to pop him upside the head, but thought better of it. She rolled her eyes and turned the radio back on. When she glanced down at her broken nail, she got heated all over again. She took out her cell phone and made a call. Monica talked about Savon to her girlfriend like he wasn't even there, and she didn't care that he heard every word she said.

When they made it home, Monica jumped out of the truck and went inside before Savon had a chance to turn off the engine. He couldn't take any more of her mouth right now, so it's a good thing she got out. What a nightmare. Savon turned on his playlist and reclined in the seat. One thing Monica had said was true: he wasn't ready to marry her.

The reason Savon hadn't called off the engagement already, had to do with him being confused. He didn't know what he wanted anymore. Even with all of her flaws and drama, Savon believed that Monica wouldn't try to drain his bank account if their marriage didn't work out. And neither of them wanted kids, so that meant he would never be stuck paying thousands of dollars in court costs and child support. Those were the big reasons why she had been chosen to wear his ring.

A man in Savon's position could have any woman he wanted. But he wanted a woman with something more to offer than just a hot body and a pretty face. Monica had all those qualities plus she had a successful career, but her attitude sucked. He needed to be able to talk to his woman—and agree to disagree. But things didn't work that way with Monica. And that frustrated the heck out of him.

Twenty minutes later, Savon got himself together and went inside to take his bashing like a man. Monica had a suitcase in hand descending the staircase, and one in the foyer when he walked through the door.

"Where are you going?" he said.

"Back to Atlanta," said Monica, pulling her bags to the front door to wait for the cab she'd called.

"Can we talk about this?" Savon reached for her arm.

"Talk? Now you want to talk?" Monica jerked her arm away and slapped his face. "I'm not talking to you. You play too many games. I thought we were moving forward tonight. And to think—I even apologized to your sorry behind." Monica gritted her teeth and stepped closer. "Go talk to that thirsty home wrecker you can't stop dealing with—I'm outta here." She put on her coat and stood by the door.

"Don't hit me again," said Savon, his eyes like slits. "I'm sick of your drama. If you walk out on me this time, don't think about coming back." With that, he turned and went upstairs.

"I hate you!" Monica shouted through tears. She fumbled to pull off her engagement ring, and then threw it at him. The five-carat diamond hit the back of Savon's neck, but he never turned around.

In his bedroom, Savon felt a headache coming on. He couldn't believe Monica had slapped him. If she hadn't been so selfish and immature, another woman could never have gotten so close to him. If she wanted to leave—deuces, two fingers. But he wouldn't be calling her to come back this time.

Chapter 13

Had Savon and Monica been at the charity event the entire time? When Bobbi had noticed Savon, their eyes locked and then so did hers and Monica's.

When Monica stood up, Bobbi had prepared herself for a confrontation because she didn't know if wacko would come to her table trying to start some mess. But she had been stunned to see Monica throw a drink in Savon's face. Thank goodness Tony didn't have a clue to the madness unfolding that could've very well ended up at their table.

On the ride home from the event, Bobbi knew she wouldn't be inviting Tony inside for a nightcap. He'd been frisky all night and she knew what that meant. But after seeing Savon and the way he'd looked at her before chasing after Monica, she wasn't in the mood for Tony's touch.

Not long after Bobbi fell asleep, her phone rang. She rubbed her eyes and picked up.

"Yes?"

Savon hesitated. Now that he had Bobbi on the line, he didn't know if he'd made the right decision.

"Savon. I know you didn't call me this late to breathe heavy in my ear."

"Yeah, uhh . . . what's up?" he said.

"For real? I'm asleep, Savon. Correction—I was asleep." If he had something to say, he'd better spit it out or get off her phone. Bobbi had no patience with people who beat around the bush, especially not exes.

"I apologize for waking you—but whatever happened to answering the telephone with hello?"

"You act like it's one in the afternoon." Bobbi yawned and sat up. "I already knew it was you. Why are you calling me?"

Savon chuckled. "Okay, Bobbi. I guess you have a point." He liked this woman. "I have some things I want to say to you, if you're willing to listen."

Her right eyebrow arched. "Okay." She drew her knees up to her chest and got comfortable.

For a good while, Savon told Bobbi about his relationship with Monica, that they'd been engaged for a year, but had yet to set a date for the wedding. The plan had been for him to get settled with his new team, and then they'd decide if the wedding would be in Atlanta or DC. But the paternity issue happened and their plans fell apart after that.

Bobbi remained silent, and Savon continued. He told Bobbi that, when he saw her at the charity event tonight, he'd realized that she was the woman for him and he wanted the opportunity to really get to know her. He said that he and Monica were officially done, and then he asked Bobbi his burning question.

"So . . . was dude at the event someone you're serious about?"

Bobbi chuckled to herself. He'd gone through darn near thirty minutes of talking about Monica just to ask about Tony.

"His name is Tony, and he's a good friend," said Bobbi. This was Savon's confession hour, not hers.

"Okay." Savon didn't know if he should believe Bobbi. With his own eyes, he saw the man kiss her and how happy she looked when he did. But Savon would find out soon enough if Bobbi were available, because he had plans to turn up the heat. He wanted to see just what kind of woman Bobbi Farqua could be to him.

———

Could Savon really be the caring, sensitive man he kept showing her? Bobbi hoped so, as she lay on his chest with a crap-eating grin plastered on her face.

After a month of dating, Savon had chosen New Year's Eve to tell her that he wanted to be exclusive. He wanted them to see if they could work in a committed relationship. So many thoughts had passed through her mind last night when he poured out his heart to her over dinner. At first, she'd hesitated because to say yes would mean she had to let her guard all the way down, and trusting him petrified her. But how could she say no?

After Bobbi agreed to be exclusive, they had consummated the relationship, all night long. It reminded her of their first encounter months ago. One orgasm after the next had wracked her body while he talked to her above a whisper about his plans for their future. Just the memory of it made her quiver.

Bobbi stretched and caught a whiff of her armpits. Her nose twitched. Then she smelled Savon's pits and her neck jerked back so hard, she almost fell off the bed.

"Get up, bae," said Bobbi, caressing Savon's chest. "We need a shower."

His grip tightened around her. "Go back to sleep," he mumbled.

Bobbi scooted out of bed and pulled at his arm, but Savon didn't budge. She needed to feel fresh if they were going to be all over each other, and he needed to get his stinky pits in the shower too. So Bobbi put her tongue in his ear, which she'd just learned this morning he hated, and he sat straight up.

"Why'd you do that?" Savon said, wiping the wetness from his ear. "I told you I don't like it."

"I'm sorry, babe." Bobbi made a sad face and laughed. "Now, get up big baby so we can freshen up." She lifted up the covers. "You smell that? You stink."

Savon jumped out of bed and chased Bobbi to the bathroom. They teased each other for a minute then she turned on the shower and they stepped in.

Bobbi swatted at Savon. "Stop," she said.

He smacked her butt again. This time, it really sounded off as the warm water rolled down her backside.

"Stop playin'." Bobbi stepped away from Savon and his manhood. They'd been at it for hours and she needed a break.

"I can't help it," he said, kissing the back of her neck. He grabbed her around the waist and pulled her back to him. "I can't get enough of you."

Bobbi gave in as both of his hands touched and teased her most sensitive places. She turned around and Savon lifted her up and she wrapped her legs around his waist. He drove them both to the brink and they released together. Then Savon lost his footing and slipped on the wet tile, causing Bobbi to land on top of him.

"Are you okay?" she said, laughing and pushing back wavy, wet locks from her face.

"Do you know who I am?" Savon beat his chest. "I take harder hits on the field."

<hr/>

"United Airlines 1507 with service to Washington, DC, now boarding at gate twelve," announced the flight attendant.

Monica handed her boarding pass to the attendant and made her way down the ramp. She tucked her tote bag underneath the seat in front of her and buckled up for the two-hour flight to confront her past.

When Savon came to Atlanta for Christmas, he hadn't bothered to come see her or call. By now, everyone knew they were no longer an item, but he'd made it painfully clear that he'd moved on.

Monica's family blamed her for the breakup, saying that she'd run Savon off with her mouth. Of course, Monica knew her attitude needed work and that she had jealous tendencies, but how could she be secure in a relationship when some new woman was always in her man's face?

Nonetheless, Monica never thought Savon would give up on her. They'd been through trying times before and managed to stay together, but the last six months had been the worst. Monica had ended the engagement because she believed that Savon had cheated on her with that tramp Bobbi. Yet being without him wasn't an option. Monica couldn't imagine her life without Savon.

As the plane taxied down the runway for takeoff, Monica couldn't remember the last time she and Savon had spent time together doing something fun. That needed to change. If Savon gave her another chance, he would not regret it. She would show him the new and improved Monica—the happy and carefree girl he'd met years ago. Monica blushed, imagining herself in Savon's arms, later tonight.

At the airport in DC, Monica picked up a rental and headed for Savon's house. They hadn't spoken since their fight over a month ago, but she wouldn't let that stop her from going after what she wanted.

At 10:00 AM, Monica pulled into Savon's driveway and went to knock on the door. Her heart raced. She took a deep, calming breath and put a hand on her stomach to settle the flutters.

When Savon didn't answer, Monica tried looking through the privacy glass windows on either side of the heavy wooden door, but she couldn't see anything. She pulled her jacket together and glanced up and down the street. She couldn't stand there waiting forever, so she used her key and went inside.

She called out to Savon above a whisper, closing the door behind her. When he didn't answer, she tiptoed through the rooms on the ground level looking for any sign of him, and then she went to the garage.

Seeing his Escalade caused the flutters to come back. But she couldn't help but wonder when he'd bought the white Benz parked next to it.

Padding up the staircase, Monica heard the television playing in Savon's bedroom. She stopped midway the stairs. Her heart pounded wildly and she found it difficult to manage her breathing. After a minute, she steadied herself and pressed forward. Monica took a deep breath and eased her head into Savon's bedroom door.

Chapter 14

Savon lay in bed, channel surfing, while Bobbi blow-dried her hair. He couldn't believe how things were happening between them. To his surprise, the sex had gone to a whole other level last night. The corners of his lips turned up at the thought, and he moved his free hand to rest in his boxers.

Bobbi finished her hair, put on a fuchsia negligee and joined Savon in bed.

"You are so sexy," he said.

"I already know that," Bobbi said, smiling.

Savon shook his head. "And cocky." He loved that about her.

"Nope—confident. Just move over, big head."

What the . . . Savon jumped up and grabbed his gun from the nightstand and motioned for Bobbi to go in the bathroom. Nodding frantically, her eyes darting between him and the gun, Bobbi followed his instructions. Then Savon chambered a round.

When his bedroom door opened wider, he saw what looked like a head leaning in and his Glock greeted the intruder.

"Savon!" said Monica, staring down the barrel of his personal security guard.

"Monica? What are you doing in my house?!" Savon lowered the gun.

Monica could hear her heartbeat above the sound of the TV. "I . . . I tried calling and knocking on the door but you didn't answer, so," she swallowed hard, "I used my key."

Savon snapped. "Used your key?! Why would you do that? I told you it was over when you left."

"I'm sorry for showing up without calling first, but we need to talk. That's why I'm here," said Monica. She tried to sound calm, but on the inside, a wave of fear threatened to overtake her.

Savon cleared his weapon and put it back in the nightstand. He plopped down on the bed needing to recover from the adrenaline rush, and then he remembered that Bobbi was in the bathroom. He rubbed his head and looked toward the ceiling. He could use divine intervention right about now.

"I've moved on. It's over. You shouldn't have come."

When Bobbi heard Savon's words, she took a deep breath and reached for the doorknob. Although she hated being in this predicament, the time had come for her to deal with Monica.

"Are you serious?" said Monica, when Bobbi came out of the bathroom. "How could you, Savon? I knew you were sleeping with that tramp. Look at her," Monica frowned, "with barely anything on."

Monica spit in Bobbi's direction and then charged Savon. But she stumbled over a shoe, tumbling onto the bed and missed him. Her breaths were long and hard, and she had an untamable look in her eyes. She got up and went after Savon again, her arms swinging out of control and making contact this time.

"Stop it, Monica." Savon grabbed her by the wrists so she couldn't move.

"Let me go," she demanded through clenched teeth. Tears stained her face.

"If I let you go, you have to stop hitting me," he said.

"Yeah . . . whatever," said Monica.

When Savon let her go, she went to pick up his cell phone and then threw it at him. He raised his arm just in time to protect his face. Then Monica went over to his dresser, and with one sweep of her hand, sent two vases crashing to the floor.

"Man . . . you better get out of my house before I lose it on you . . ." said Savon.

He closed the distance between them when Monica picked up a crystal picture frame from his mother, and ripped it from her fingers. He grabbed both of her arms again and held them tight. "That's it! If you break one more thing in my house—"

"Yeah, yeah. What are you gonna do?" She cut him off. "You know what? You're a sorry, no good for nothing cheater." Monica twisted her arms. "Let me go!"

Savon's eyes were red with anger and he tightened his grip on her.

"Ouch!" Monica squirmed. "You're hurting me."

Savon let her go. And before his hands could drop to his sides, Monica had picked up the crystal frame and hurled it at the wall, leaving a hole and shards of crystal on the floor.

Savon sat back on the bed and released a heavy sigh. He took calming breaths to settle himself so he wouldn't lose control. He didn't want to put hands on Monica but he could only take so much, and she had pushed him to his limit.

Monica got back in Savon's face. "I knew you were sleeping with her. But you kept denying it. That home wrecking, hussy." Monica looked at Bobbi and turned up her nose.

Bobbi's fists clenched, but she didn't say anything. If Monica brought all that fervor across the room to take a swing at her, her modeling career would be over. And before she could finish her thought, Monica came toward her and they stood toe to toe.

"Why can't you find your own man, huh?" said Monica, pointing in Bobbi's face.

Bobbi could smell the stale coffee on Monica's breath, but she still didn't say a word.

"You low self esteem having trick. Savon is mine. Get your own man."

When Savon heard that, he jumped up and got between them.

"Move, Savon!" Monica stepped around him and got back in Bobbi's face. "What's wrong? You only talk to men at restaurants?" Monica sucked her teeth. "Get this bit—"

Crack! Before she knew it, Bobbi had tagged Monica upside her big head and she dropped to the floor.

"Whoaa!" said Savon, looking at Bobbi. He bent down to check Monica's breathing. "What did you do?"

"What?!" said Bobbi. "I know you're not asking me anything about that raggedy chicken head. You should be asking me how I'm doing." Bobbi massaged her knuckles. "I could care less if she takes another breath."

Bobbi stepped over Monica's limp body and went to the bathroom. She sat on the commode fighting back tears. Her main purpose for leaving the bathroom earlier, after hearing Monica's voice, had been to keep Savon honest. She wanted Monica to know they were a couple now—she wanted to rub it in her face. But Bobbi hadn't expected it to come to physical blows.

Savon paced the floor. When Bobbi came out of the bathroom, he stared at her for a moment, and then rolled his eyes. "I checked her pulse. Thank goodness she's still alive," he said. "You didn't have to hit her like that."

"Are you on her side?" said Bobbi. "You saw how she disrespected me. She'd better be glad I didn't punch her in her throat and put her big head to sleep for real."

Savon didn't know how to respond. He hadn't seen this side of Bobbi. He didn't realize she could be a fighter in this way or that she would even consider "putting someone to sleep" as she said.

Savon pointed down at Monica to make his point. "She's on the floor, unconscious. Do you see that? Man!" He brushed past Bobbi to the other side of the room and punched the wall. His fist went through the drywall and he pulled out blood stained knuckles.

Bobbi spun around when she heard the impact. "Let me get this straight," she said. "You asked me to be your woman . . . then she comes to town unexpectedly, beats up on you, and then gets up in my face calling me names, and I'm supposed to take it? Is this what comes with being in a relationship with you?"

Savon looked at her from the corners of his eyes.

"I asked you a question!" said Bobbi.

He waved her off, and winced at the pain in this injured hand.

"Unbelievable." Bobbi went to the bathroom and filled a glass with water. Then went back into the bedroom, looked at Savon, and poured the water on Monica's face.

"Are you crazy?!" Savon rushed over to Bobbi and snatched the glass from her hand.

"No, you're the crazy one!" said Bobbi. She couldn't remember a time when she'd been so unsettled. She wanted to kick Monica and fight Savon. He had the gall to ask if she was crazy, when in fact, she was the only sane person in the room.

Just then, Monica began mumbling and calling for Savon. Bobbi watched as he went to her and kneeled down to help her up off the floor. Humph. These two deserved each other. Bobbi shook her head. She got dressed and packed her things while Savon catered to Monica.

He helped her to the bed and she reached for her throbbing head. When Monica realized that Bobbi was still there, she used all the energy she could muster to call Bobbi the B-word. And before she could blink her eyes, Bobbi was standing over her.

"Looka here," said Bobbi. "I tried to let you and Savon handle your drama, but you won't leave me out of it. Keep running that mouth of yours and you'll be kissing the carpet again!" Bobbi got in her face eyeball to eyeball. "Got it?"

Savon stood up, grabbing Bobbi by the shoulders. He walked her backwards and away from Monica. "You need to leave," he said. "This is not working. I need to figure things out and I can't do that with you here." He looked back at Monica and sighed. "Look at the mess you made."

"So you're saying this is my fault?"

"Please, just leave, Bobbi."

"I can't believe you!" Bobbi held back tears as she snatched up her overnight bag and stormed out of the room.

Savon went downstairs to let Bobbi out, but she'd already gone. He watched her speed down the street from the open garage. How had his fresh start to the New Year ended like this? Monica should never have come, but at the same time, Bobbi should've kept her cool. He still couldn't believe she'd hit Monica. Now he had to take her to the hospital and risk more public scrutiny. Some publicist.

Savon walked around his Escalade checking for scratches and flats, and then closed the garage door and went back upstairs. All he wanted to do was play football and live a quiet life with an amazing woman. Was that too much to ask?

He found Monica in the bathroom looking at the indent in the bridge of her nose. Gently rubbing her finger over it, she cried. Savon embraced her and apologized for what had happened. She looked up at him, worn down from the battle, and sobbed for a good while.

"I need to take you to the emergency room," he said.

"I know."

Chapter 15

The nerve of Savon to put her out! Tears blurred Bobbi's vision as she merged into traffic. She took a shaky hand from the steering wheel and wiped at her eyes. Images of Monica and Savon in his bedroom flashed before her and she felt it in her heart. How could he!

Bobbi drove around aimlessly, uncertain of her next move. She just wanted the pain to stop. Going home and being alone would only make her feel worse. But she didn't want anyone to see her like this. Thirty minutes later, she found herself knocking on Nikki's front door.

"Hey . . . what's going on?" said Nikki. "I didn't know you were coming over."

Bobbi brushed past her with no greeting at all and went to sit on the sofa.

Nikki closed the door. "What's wrong?"

Bobbi looked at Nikki, and then reached for one of the decorative pillows beside her and covered her face.

"Is everything okay? Is the family okay?" blurted Nikki.

Bobbi nodded, and Nikki breathed a sigh of relief. But when Bobbi moved the pillow from her face, Nikki rushed over and sat next to her friend.

"It's okay, sweetie. Talk to me. What's going on?"

Bobbi couldn't hold back the tears any longer. She fell into Nikki's arms and wept. Savon's hurtful words, and the way he'd treated her, had broken her heart. The tears wouldn't stop falling.

Nikki comforted Bobbi without another word. She rocked Bobbi in her arms until the sobs turned into an occasional sniffle.

Once Bobbi got her self together, she told Nikki everything. It hurt so bad knowing that Savon had chosen Monica over her, especially after she'd convinced her self to trust him.

Bobbi didn't leave Nikki's house until late that evening. And when she did, Nikki made her promise to go to church with her tomorrow, no matter how she felt or how big the bags under her eyes would be by morning.

At home, Bobbi mulled over her fight with Monica. She didn't regret defending herself, but she hadn't meant to knock the girl unconscious. When Monica had gotten up in her face with all the aggressive behavior and name-calling, Bobbi had snapped. Her "friend or foe" military training had kicked in and Monica got handled like a foe. But what a relief it had been to hear Monica's slurred words when she came to.

Nonetheless, Bobbi still couldn't process Savon's behavior. Hours before Monica had showed up, they were in love. And now he acted like he didn't care at all. Bobbi needed to understand why he'd switched up on her. So she pulled up his number and called.

Savon tensed up when he saw the number. "Hello," he said in a snippy tone. He didn't want to talk to Bobbi, but not answering might give her the idea to stop by his house later and he couldn't chance that.

"Hey," said Bobbi, above a whisper.

"What's up?"

"Uhm . . . I wanted to talk about what happened earlier. I feel like you blame me."

"Look. I know Monica was wrong, but you took things to another level when you hit her. You broke her nose." Savon got louder, and a family sitting in the waiting room whispered to each other, darting glances at him. He noticed and lowered his voice. "Now I'm sitting here in the hospital looking like a woman beater or something." *Man!*

"Humph. Whether you want to face it or not, this whole thing is your fault." Bobbi raised her voice too. "Obviously she didn't know y'all were done or she wouldn't have popped up on you—from Atlanta! So this mess that you want to blame on me, is your own fault! Your communication sucks and that's why you're in the ER."

"You know what? I'm done," said Savon. He got up and walked toward the red exit sign. "Don't call me again."

Bobbi pressed the end-call button on her cell phone five times and threw it across the bed. She turned off the lights and cried herself to sleep.

At eight o'clock Sunday morning, Nikki pulled into Bobbi's driveway. Bobbi had just come out of the bathroom when she heard the knock at the door. She opened the blinds and saw Nikki standing there, hands on her hips, looking back at her. Bobbi laughed and motioned that she would be right down.

"What took you so long to answer the door, girl? It's cold as I-don't-know-what out here." Nikki walked past Bobbi, rubbing her hands together on the way to the kitchen. "Where's the coffee?"

"You didn't say you were coming this early," said Bobbi, starting the coffeemaker. "I don't feel like going to church today. Look at my eyes. I look like I lost a fight."

Nikki pulled off her coat and draped it over the bar stool next to her. Bobbi was right about her eyes. But Nikki ignored her comment. They were going to church even if she had to apply an entire tube of concealer to those puffy bags.

"I'll do your makeup," said Nikki. "All you need to do is get dressed so we can get out of here by nine-thirty. Can you handle that?"

Bobbi rolled her eyes. "Okay . . . okay." As much as she didn't feel like going, she didn't want to hear Nikki's mouth.

Bobbi hadn't been to a brick and mortar house of prayer in over two years. But she had been a faithful member at bedside Baptist. Even when she worked on Sundays, she still streamed her favorite eService on her laptop.

When they pulled into the church parking lot, Nikki told Bobbi about Ruth, a community outreach counselor who happened to be a member of the church. She told Bobbi that she'd arranged for them to talk after the service.

Bobbi frowned. "What? Why did you do that?"

"Because I think she can help you get to a better place with this whole Savon thing."

"If I had known you were going to pull this, I would have stayed my Black behind at home." Bobbi turned her head and looked out the window.

Nikki touched her arm. "Look, B. You went through some pretty heavy stuff yesterday. And I just wanna make sure you're okay—that's all."

"Humph." Bobbi pulled down the sun visor and checked her makeup. She couldn't be mad at Nikki for wanting to help.

Nikki went on to tell Bobbi that she'd met Ruth while she was in undergrad. Sister Ruth had held a weekly session at a nearby community center, where she talked to young women about healthy relationships with men. This piqued Bobbi's curiosity.

"So why am I just hearing about this Ruth person if you've known her this long?"

"Because I only went to a couple of her meetings. Shucks, you know we thought we knew everything back then." Nikki laughed. "But seriously, I hear she's good to talk to and gives great advice."

Bobbi didn't think Ruth could tell her anything she didn't already know about men. Everybody knows that men lie to get what they want. And Bobbi had the remedy for that—just don't trust them. But, what the heck—if nothing else, maybe she would get a good laugh out of it.

"I'll let you know after church if I want to go through with it," said Bobbi.

"Fair enough," said Nikki as they walked through the double doors of the church.

Bobbi stood to her feet, clapping and singing along with the choir during praise and worship. Every song spoke to her pain in a different way and she cried out, "Yes, Lord," with her hands lifted high. When the pastor got up to preach, his words of comfort caused the same reaction and she dabbed at the corners of her eyes during the sermon. By the time the service had ended, so had Bobbi's energy. But she didn't want to disappoint Nikki, so she followed her downstairs to a classroom where they found Ruth conversing with another woman.

When the woman left, Ruth waved Nikki and Bobbi in, and greeted them with a warm hug. Bobbi liked her sleek chignon and the classic but fashionable wool suit she wore with a single strand of pearls. Ruth had a regal vibe about her.

"So, Bobbi," said Ruth, "Nikki tells me that you're going through a rough period in a relationship. I'd like to talk with you about that, if it's okay?"

"Sure." Bobbi forced a smile.

"Let's go have a seat over here," Ruth said, pointing and walking toward a table in the corner.

Bobbi lagged behind waving good-bye to Nikki, but under her breath, she pleaded with her not to leave. Nikki snickered and closed the door.

Sister Ruth didn't waste any time digging into the matter. "So, tell me what happened this weekend that has Nikki so concerned about you, young lady." Ruth smiled.

Bobbi uncrossed her legs and sat back in the chair. She told Ruth about Savon and how they'd agreed to be in an exclusive relationship yesterday morning, and then his ex-fiancée showed up looking for trouble. "Long story short," said Bobbi, "somehow Savon decided that the whole mess was my fault, and he asked me to leave his house while he catered to his ex." Bobbi sniffled, reaching in her purse for tissues.

"And what did you do?"

"I left. What else could I do? He stood in my face and asked me to leave, while his ex sat there looking crazy." Bobbi rolled her eyes. "She'd better be glad all I did was punch her," Bobbi mumbled.

Ruth's eyes stretched wide. "Okay. Well, that's more than enough to be upset about. So, what do you think about how Savon treated you?"

Bobbi's bottom lip quivered. "I hate the way he treated me."

Sister Ruth pushed back from the table and went around to where Bobbi sat and embraced her. "Look at me, Bobbi," she said, lifting her chin. "I can help you find peace in the midst of this turmoil if you'll be transparent with me. Can you do that?"

Bobbi wiped her nose. "Ahh—okay. I'll try." Bobbi stiffened. How much more transparent did she need to be?

Thirty minutes later, Nikki knocked on the door and stuck her head inside. "You ready, B?"

"If it's okay with Bobbi," Ruth blurted, "I'll take her home when we finish."

Bobbi wanted to scream. "Uhm . . . okay." She forced a smile toward Ruth and cut her eye at Nikki when Ruth looked away.

Without the need to rush, Ruth asked Bobbi about her past. She wanted to know what her relationships with men were like before Savon.

Bobbi told Ruth that in most of her relationships she'd been cheated on, lied to, or taken advantage of. Then Bobbi admitted that she didn't believe in love anymore. "Love hurts," she said. "I don't have it in me anymore to keep going down that same road, wanting and expecting things to be different the next time around."

"I see," said Ruth. Hearing Bobbi say those things saddened her. "Did you grow up with your father?"

"Not really. I saw him every now and then."

"Did you feel loved by him?"

"Uhm . . . not really. Why?" Bobbi locked eyes with the counselor.

"Well, dear," said Ruth, "sometimes there can be lingering emotions from past life experiences, and I want to make sure you're telling yourself the truth about love." Ruth reached in her tote bag and handed Bobbi a pen and pad for her to write down her home address and phone number. Then she handed Bobbi her business card and said, "I'm here if you want to cry about Savon or talk about anything. Call me anytime."

"Thank you." Bobbi managed a smile. She looked at the picture of Ruth on the card and put it in her purse—thankful the intervention had ended.

The next day, Bobbi worked from home. She needed time to get her emotions in check. She called her assistant and rattled off a list of tasks for Ciara to complete for the week, and requested that she set up video calls in place of her scheduled meetings.

By mid-day, Bobbi gave up on trying to focus on her work. Images of Savon putting her out and taking Monica's side tormented her. And, to top it off, Sister Ruth had messed up her head by bringing up her father and saying absolutely nothing about her drama with Savon.

Bobbi went downstairs and poured a glass of lemonade. She walked over to the kitchen window and pulled up the shade. She couldn't help but think about what happened over the weekend. Savon had played her. He hadn't wanted a committed relationship. He just wanted more sex. She wiped at a lone tear.

Awhile later, Bobbi called Ciara back and told her not to forward any more calls, but to take messages and she would respond tomorrow.

"Oh . . . before we hang up," said Ciara. "Lance came by. I told him you were working from home all week, but he didn't leave a message.

"Thanks, Ciara."

Next, Bobbi called Nikki. She wanted to get out of the house. Hanging with her best friend might be all the therapy she needed.

"What's up, B?" said Nikki.

"That's not the professional way to answer a phone when you're at work," Bobbi teased.

"B, your name and number came up on the caller-id. What do you want me to do? Act like I don't know it's you?"

"Whatever, girl. Look . . . you wanna do dinner tonight?"

"Sure." Nikki covered the mouthpiece while she talked to a colleague who entered her office. "I have to go. I'll pick you up at six?"

"Okay. I'm working from home. Bye."

Later that night at the restaurant, Bobbi and Nikki talked about family stuff and sipped on hot chocolate. Bobbi knew that Nikki wanted to hear about her meeting with Sister Ruth, but she just couldn't go there right now. Last night, she'd been asleep when Nikki called, so they hadn't had a chance to talk about it. But Bobbi desperately needed peace, and talking about Savon wouldn't get her to that place.

Nikki mentioned going to Atlanta for the MLK holiday and to the Warriors playoff game the following weekend. She tried to bring Bobbi out of her funk and put a smile on her face, but nothing helped.

"I'm going to the restroom," Bobbi said, scooting out of the booth.

"Okay." Nikki frowned as Bobbi walked off.

In the restroom, Bobbi washed her hands and rubbed them dry under the blower. When she pulled the door handle to leave, a rosy-cheeked toddler with sandy brown pigtails stumbled inside.

"Whoa," said Bobbi, reaching out to stop the little one from falling. "You okay?"

"Please excuse her," said the lady who came in right after. "She ran off without me."

Bobbi smiled. "Oh, that's okay. I needed to slow down too."

The woman smiled back and took the child into a stall.

On the way back to the table, Bobbi took five steps and paused. Tony stood at the hostess stand with his arm around the waist of a woman who could be her stunt double. The lady had a small waist and curves, long black hair and honey kissed skin just like her. It didn't look like a first date either. Even though her mind insisted that Tony was only a friend, her heart felt betrayed.

Bobbi sighed. Looking over at the table where Nikki sat, she couldn't avoid walking past the entrance. So, she calmed herself, arched her back—put on her game face and pressed forward.

"Hi Tony." Bobbi touched his arm and smiled at him and his date.

"What's up, Bobbi?" he said. He gave her a quick hug and pecked her cheek.

"Tasha, I'd like you to meet a very good friend of mine . . . Bobbi Farqua."

"Nice to meet you, Tasha," said Bobbi, smiling.

"Same here." Tasha smiled back.

"Well," said Bobbi, "I'd better get back to my table. She pointed to the right. "Good seeing you." She looked at Tony. "And a pleasure meeting you, Tasha."

Bobbi choked back tears. Was that all she'd been to Tony—a good friend? Although she knew it to be true, somehow it diminished what they'd shared for nearly three years.

"What's the matter?" said Nikki, noticing the tears.

"Nothing. I'm just being emotional." Bobbi blinked to push the tears out and then brushed them away. "Did you see me talking to Tony?"

"Yeah."

Bobbi looked at her plate. "I've lost my appetite. Can you take me home?"

"Okay." Nikki called for their server, paid the bill and they were out.

On the ride home, Nikki left Bobbi to her thoughts. When they pulled up in Bobbi's driveway, she reached over and gave her friend a big hug. "Things will get better."

Chapter 16

The other night when Nikki had dropped her off, Bobbi had said her prayers, got in bed, and dared herself to cry. She'd been an emotional wreck long enough.

The roller coaster she'd been riding over the last week—loving Savon one minute and wanting to crack his nuts the next—had caused her to lose sight of the important day-to-day tasks of her personal life. But today she would get back on track. Bobbi got up from her home desk, and went outside to check the mail.

She sorted through it at the kitchen table, putting the bills in the basket on the counter, and the junk mail in the garbage. Bobbi opened the pink envelope from Ruth Abernathy, and admired the handwritten note. It read:

Dear Bobbi:

You are loveable. It is a lie to believe that love doesn't matter. Of course love matters. We were built for love. Nothing about this life we live is any good without it.

You are a beautiful woman, and clearly you take very good care of yourself on the outside. But how is your heart? My dear, a broken heart must be healed. And believe it or not, a good way to start is through forgiveness. You can't change the past, but you can decide to forgive the men that have hurt you, including Savon. Let's explore this when you're ready.

Here is a Bible passage I want you to make time to read daily: Love is patient and kind. Love is not jealous or boastful or proud or rude. It does not demand its own way. It is not irritable, and it keeps no record of being wronged. It does not rejoice about injustice but rejoices whenever the truth wins out. Love never gives up, never loses faith, is always hopeful, and endures through every circumstance. 1 Corinthians 13:4–7 (NLT)

Bobbi, this is the definition and demonstration of love. It is how God loves you. These verses will teach you how to love, and how to recognize love when it comes your way.

It matters to God that you're hurting. Please call me whenever you want to talk.

With love,
Sister Ruth

Tears stained the pages of the letter as Ruth's words pierced Bobbi's heart. She read the Bible verses a couple more times and put the letter back in the envelope. Moments later, she went back upstairs to work, but her efforts were futile.

Three things in her past weighed heavy on her heart: feelings about her absent father, being sexually assaulted as a teenager, and her first experience with an unfaithful man. How could she forgive all of that? By nightfall, Bobbi had a headache. She'd spent hours trying to analyze her life and all the mistakes she'd made. She realized she couldn't work through this by herself.

Bobbi eyed the clock on the nightstand and picked up the phone to call Ruth. But after pressing the first three digits of her number, she changed her mind and went downstairs instead to watch television.

An hour later, the telephone rang.

"Yes?"

"Bobbi. Is that you, dear?"

"Sister Ruth?" *What the—*

"Yes, it's me. Did you get my letter?" Ruth said.

"I did," said Bobbi. "I wanted to call you, but I thought it was too late."

"I probably should be in bed earlier," Ruth chuckled, "but I'm usually up until ten or ten thirty most nights." She changed the subject. "Do you want to talk about the letter now, or some other time?"

"Now is fine." Bobbi sat up on the sofa. "I'm still processing everything, but the forgiveness piece is hard. I believe in love with family and friends . . . just not with men. In my experience, they lie and cheat just for the sake of lying and cheating."

"Yes, forgiveness can be hard, but it's more for you than the other person. So you can be free from any bitterness, fear, or rejection that can influence your life today," said Ruth. "And even if it's an accurate statement that men lie—it's the lies you tell yourself and believe that will always have a greater impact on the quality of your life." Ruth heard soft sniffles on the line. She continued, "Don't give up on love, Bobbi. It will find you one day. You'll see."

"Okay," said Bobbi above a whisper. "I have to go now. I'll talk to you later."

"Good night, dear. I'll check on you soon. Oh . . . and don't forget to pray."

Through tears, Bobbi pressed the end-call button. She blew her nose and snuggled under the leopard print throw on the sofa and prayed.

Father God, please help me understand how to forgive and how to even care about trusting a man again. I'm sick of the lies and I'm sick of getting hurt . . . I don't need it. And, God, please show me what lies I'm telling myself. Help me, God. In Jesus's name. Amen. And bless Sister Ruth. Amen.

Saturday morning, Bobbi returned home from a kickboxing class with Nikki. She showered and threw a load of laundry in the washing machine, and then pulled out her laptop to put the final touches on an endorsement deal pitch for Sweet Feet.

Her phone rang and she winced when she saw Lance's name on the screen. He'd called and left a message two days ago, but she hadn't listened to it yet.

"Hello."

"So you are alive," Lance teased.

Bobbi laughed. "I am. Just been working from home all week. I needed a change of scenery."

"Yeah, your assistant told me. But I wanted to make sure you were okay. I saw you at church Sunday, then you weren't at work, and you didn't respond to my call, so I thought I might have to come to your house and lay eyes on you."

Bobbi gave a nervous chuckle, wondering if he would really come to her house uninvited. "Well, as you can see—or shall I say hear—all is well. But you said you saw me at church?"

"Yeah, at New Covenant Believers Church in Chantilly. I've been going there for about three months. I saw you walk in with another lady, but I didn't see you after service."

"Oh, okay, uh . . . I had something to do afterward, so I didn't hang around."

"So—" he said, changing the subject, "you wanna get lunch one day next week?"

"Uh, sure," said Bobbi, biting down on her finger. "When I get back in the office and see what's going on, I'll let you know which day works best for me."

"Fair enough. I'll talk to you then. Enjoy the rest of your weekend," said Lance.

"I will. And thanks for checking on me." Bobbi smiled. "Bye."

Bobbi hung up the phone and played back Lance's voice message from Thursday. The concern in his voice touched her. She played the message three times, deciding then to make time for Lance next week.

The following Tuesday, Lance and Bobbi met in the lobby of their building to go to lunch. Bobbi joked with him as he opened the door of his silver Maserati for her.

"Well, dang. The cyber security business must be booming. This is nice," she said.

Lance chuckled, closing the door. When he got inside, he said, "It's my weekend car. But I pulled it out just for you."

Bobbi smiled, ignoring his last comment. "So tell me about your business."

Lance told Bobbi that he started his business ten years ago as an independent consultant and the demand for his expertise had made it necessary to hire employees and grow the company. Moving to the DC area had been a power move to expand even more with government contracts.

The more details Lance shared about his business successes during lunch, the more intrigued Bobbi became. She knew how hard it was to start and maintain a lucrative company. So she respected his hustle.

Sitting next to him at the sushi bar, Bobbi laughed at his almost funny but-not-quite sense of humor. She hadn't noticed it before, but Lance had the cutest dimple in his chin.

In the days that followed, Bobbi had found a new friend in Lance. After that first lunch, they had gone bowling after work. They had so much fun hanging out, that they scheduled at least one day every week to link up for lunch or whatever else they wanted to do. Lance would share stories about his clients and crazy experiences, and Bobbi even told him about her first meeting with Sweet Feet and his goo-goo eyes and wet lips. They joked around and laughed a lot, which helped Bobbi forget about her troubles. Lance's interest in getting to know her couldn't have come at a better time. He gave her heart a break from thinking about Savon.

One day after lunch, Bobbi went with Lance back to his office so they could finish chatting about a potential business deal. Bobbi wasn't a fan of doing official business with friends and family unless they were already well-established brands, and Lance definitely fell into that category. Then out of nowhere, Lance changed the subject and got personal.

"Are you seeing anyone," he said.

Bobbi frowned. "Uhm . . . no." The last thing Bobbi wanted to talk about was relationships.

Lance nodded and picked back up with the previous conversation.

"Oh, no you don't," said Bobbi. "You don't get to ask me that and not answer the question yourself. So are you dating?"

"Nah. I'm not dating. Ava is my priority right now—and growing my business."

"So, you can't take care of Ava and date?"

"I guess it's possible, but since my wife passed, I haven't wanted to put Ava or myself in a situation that might not last."

Bobbi covered her mouth. "I'm so sorry to hear about your loss."

"Thank you. It was hard . . . but we're okay now," said Lance.

"If you don't mind me asking, when did she pass?"

"Three years ago—in a car accident."

Bobbi moved toward Lance and embraced him before she realized it. He wrapped his arms around her waist and rested his head in her bosom as she stood over him offering her condolences. His grip tightened around her body when he felt her leg move to step away. So, she held him longer, her own heart breaking at the thought of losing someone so close.

"Well," said Bobbi, finally stepping back. She rested a hand on Lance's shoulder. "I'd better get back to my office."

"Yeah . . . you should. I'll call you later," he said.

Chapter 17

Since the day Lance and Bobbi had talked about relationships, the pace of their calls and texts had picked up. Bobbi had even told Grace how much she enjoyed Lance's company and that she'd been showing him a good time in DC.

When Bobbi introduced Lance to Nikki weeks ago, they'd hit it off right away. And tonight, the three of them, and Todd were hanging out at Indi Red celebrating Nikki's latest career move. She had partnered with an entertainment law practice to prepare for a joint business venture she and Bobbi were planning.

During dinner, the guys talked basketball—they were pumped about the Washington Magicians making it past round one in the NBA playoffs. And Bobbi and Nikki went on nonstop about their business plans almost forgetting they weren't alone.

Todd interrupted the ladies to ask a question.

"Lance and I were thinking," he said. "Y'all want to go to the playoff game Monday night?"

Nikki and Bobbi looked at each other, both wanting to say no, but not wanting to come off rude.

"Uh . . . let me check my schedule and I'll let you know," said Bobbi.

"That goes for me too, babe," said Nikki. "I'll let you know tomorrow." Nikki reached for Todd's hand.

Lance chimed in. "I guess Todd and I are the only basketball fans at the table? We thought you ladies would be excited about going to a playoff game."

"No, I like basketball," said Bobbi. "It's the crowds I don't like. And that's a work night too." The thought of being herded into the Verizon Center after work wasn't the least bit appealing.

"Yeah," said Nikki. We'll let y'all know by tomorrow."

Bobbi smiled at Lance and leaned in closer. "I'll let you know," she whispered.

Then her phone rang and the number came up private. Bobbi frowned.

"Hello."

"Uhm . . . Bobbi. It's Savon. Can we talk?"

The wide-eyed look on Bobbi's face caused everyone at the table to look at her. "I'm busy right now. I'll call you later," she blurted, and then hung up.

The last person Bobbi had expected to ring her telephone was Savon. Three months had passed since they last talked, and she'd been much better for it. She didn't want to deal with him, or any of the emotions connected to the drama he brought to her life.

But the hardest part and her biggest regret had been signing on Savon as a client. Their affair had caused Bobbi to be negligent in her PR duties and she didn't like that. Her clients could count on her—they could reach out to her at any time, day or night.

Bobbi took the time to nurture her relationships so clients would feel comfortable keeping her in the loop with the good, bad, and ugly of their lives. This helped her stay in front of issues that could impact them and their brand. Nevertheless, all things considered, she still wasn't ready to deal with Savon.

When the group left the restaurant, Lance dropped Bobbi off at home. And before she could even get in the front door, Nikki called.

"Who was that on the phone?"

"Brace yourself," said Bobbi. "Savon."

"What? What did he say?"

"That fool asked if we could talk. What in the world do we have to talk about?"

"Are you calling him back?" said Nikki.

"I don't know." Bobbi sighed. "He's my client, so I have to find a way to be mature about this. But I don't want anything to do with him anymore. I need to figure it out."

"I hear ya. You definitely have some decisions to make. Well . . . let me get off this phone and entertain my boo-boo-ski. See you at church tomorrow."

Bobbi's phone rang again after she hung up with Nikki. This time Savon didn't bother blocking his digits. She made a mental note to re-save his number in her phone: code name "Nutcracker."

Savon said hello a couple of times before Bobbi said anything. He didn't deserve her time or her breath.

"Yes, Savon?" said Bobbi at last.

"Uhm . . . Since some time has passed . . . can we have a mature conversation?"

"Now is not a good time. I'm busy."

"But I need to talk to you about my brand. I have some ideas about taking things to the next level," he said.

"Okay. I'll give you a call on Monday. Good night."

Bobbi ended the call before Savon could get another word in. She refused to talk to him on his terms. Not even about business.

As promised, Bobbi called Savon on Monday evening from work. When his voicemail kicked in, she left a message telling him that she could no longer represent him, then wished him well and hung up.

After she left the message, disappointment washed over her. That message had been downright unprofessional. But now that the call had been made, she could move on with her life. Savon wasn't her only client. She had many others to work hard for, including Sweet Feet who happened to be making My Way a lot of money right now. Besides, one baller on her roster might be all she could handle.

Later that night, in sweats with her hair in a high bun, Bobbi sat in the family room watching television. She flipped through channels, stopping at the news networks first to check for breaking stories. If her clients didn't keep her in the loop with crisis situations, the media would.

But her purpose for turning on the tube had nothing to do with work. Bobbi didn't want to think about work—or anything else, for that matter. The mindless dribble of reality TV would be her only focus until she fell asleep.

The phone rang while Bobbi talked back to the TV telling a naive female what to say to her cheating man. She looked at her phone and rejected the call.

Seconds later, it rang again. Bobbi rolled her eyes and muted the TV. It seemed like answering the phone would be the only way to get some peace.

"Hello."

"Hey, beautiful."

Is he crazy? "What is it?" said Bobbi.

"So you don't want to work with me anymore?" said Savon.

Bobbi rolled her eyes. "My plate is pretty full right now . . . plus, so much has happened between us that I don't think it's in my best interest to keep you as a client. I'm sure you can understand that."

"Okay. Well, maybe—"

Bobbi stopped Savon mid-sentence. "Look. I was doing something when you called so I have to go. But I hope you're able to find someone to take your brand to the next level. All the best."

Bobbi ended the call, unmuted the television, and reached her hand into a bag of tropical trail mix. She crunched almonds and shook her head. Savon had to be on drugs. He would not take up any more of her time with his drama.

———

After a breakfast meeting with a client the next morning, Bobbi entered the glass door of her office suite around noon. Her assistant grabbed her by the arm.

"You won't believe your office," said Ciara. "Take a deep breath and follow me."

"What's going on in my office?" said Bobbi. "Is someone in there? You know I don't like anyone in my office without my knowledge."

"Calm down. No one is in your office. Just follow me. And close your eyes."

Bobbi didn't like it, but she trusted Ciara, so she went along with her instructions. Ciara ushered Bobbi past the reception desk and into her private office space.

"You can open your eyes now."

Bobbi's face lit up. "When did this happen? Who are they from?" She sat her purse on the desk and then checked the card in one of the bouquets. "Savon?"

"We had three deliveries this morning," said Ciara, with her hands on her hips.

Bobbi couldn't believe her eyes. Twelve vases, each with a dozen long stem roses of varying colors: red, pink, white, yellow, coral, and even purple, monopolized her space. The sweet fragrance reminded Bobbi of springtime in her mother's garden growing up.

After Ciara left her office, Bobbi collected the cards and read them. A different apology had been handwritten on each one. Bobbi threw up her hands. She thought she'd made her feelings perfectly clear to Savon last night when he'd called. Their business dealings were over, just like their short-lived relationship. So what in the world was he up to?

Nevertheless, Bobbi had waited a long time for an apology. So, seeing the words on each card and the abundance of roses tugged at her heart a little bit. No man had ever made such a grand gesture toward her. But it would take more than that for her to allow him back into her life. She shook her head and slid the three vases on her desk to the side so she could get some work done.

Savon followed up the floral deliveries with a call to Bobbi later that evening. She let the call go to voicemail while she talked with a media contact about Lil Dizzy. Instead of leaving a voice message, he sent a text asking her to call him.

By the time Bobbi got home from work, it was eight o'clock. She took out her phone and, for the fifth or sixth time, read the text message from Savon. She couldn't decide whether to call or text him back. Although she had expected to hear from him at some point after the elaborate rose stunt, she hadn't considered how she might respond.

She thought about all the roses decorating her office, and then the memory of Savon's insensitivity toward her with Monica overshadowed it. Bobbi dismissed Savon's request for her to call him, and replied to his text instead.

Thanks for the roses . . . they're beautiful. B

Satisfied with her response, she powered down her phone, tidied up downstairs, and went for a run on the treadmill. She wasn't prepared to carry on a conversation with Savon tonight or go back and forth with him texting.

On Wednesday, Bobbi received another dozen roses, lavender this time, and scribbled on the note, Savon had written:

Please talk to me.

This morning, when Bobbi had turned on her cell phone, she had a missed call from Savon. He'd left a voice message saying that he wanted to talk and had asked her to call him when she had time. But Bobbi had ignored that request too.

When she walked into the office on Thursday, Ciara told her that she'd had another delivery and then waved her hand toward Bobbi's office. This time, Ciara didn't get up to see Bobbi's reaction. After three days of flower deliveries, the thrill was gone.

On the center of Bobbi's desk sat a beautiful crystal vase with a bouquet of stem calla lilies in shades of amethyst, pink, and white. The card read:

Bobbi, what do you want?

Whoever Savon had consulted about flowers knew what they were doing. And the notes on the cards had helped her to forgive him, but this man wanted more than just her forgiveness.

She received a call from Savon later on that day.

"Hello," she said.

"Hey, beautiful. How are you?"

"I'm good. Uhm . . . thanks for the calla lilies. They're my favorite."

"I'm glad you like them." Savon cleared his throat. "Bobbi, I'm sorry I hurt you. Things got out of control that day and I didn't know how to handle it. I said things I didn't mean and I hurt the person I wanted to be with." He paused, and then said, "Can I come to see you?"

As Bobbi listened, her heart raced. She didn't know what to say. His words and the tenderness of his delivery got next to her. This was exactly why she wanted nothing to do with love anymore. It made her vulnerable and she didn't want to be. It tinkered with her heart and she didn't want to feel anything. She didn't want to be open to Savon. And she hated that her heart betrayed her right now.

"Hello . . . you still there?" he said.

"I'm here. But I need some time to take this in. Thank you for apologizing, though. I needed to hear that . . . and I forgive you.

About your branding ideas . . . I'll have Ciara call you later to set up an appointment."

"Okay," said Savon.

Still later that afternoon, around four o'clock, Lance got off the elevator on Bobbi's floor. He had returned from a business trip earlier that day and hadn't spoken with Bobbi since Nikki's celebration at Indi Red.

When Ciara sent him back to her office, Bobbi stood to greet him with a hug.

"Hey you, what's goin' on?" said Bobbi. With all the roses and emotional madness centered on Savon, Bobbi hadn't given much thought to Lance's whereabouts.

"Just getting back from Houston." Lance's body stiffened in her embrace as his eyes scanned the flowers that had transformed her office. "Someone must have messed up real bad to have to beg like this," he said.

Bobbi chuckled. "Yes, he did." She was surprised at Lance's physical and verbal response. She didn't understand it, but she didn't want to address it and make things more awkward.

Lance looked into Bobbi's eyes. "I'm glad to see you're okay. I'll talk to you later," he said, and then left her office.

Chapter 18

Bobbi watched Savon talk, but she'd stopped listening minutes ago. He'd come to her office to sell her on ways to expand his brand. But seeing him and his lips brought back memories, which she chose to focus on right now instead of his ideas. They'd had some good times before he ruined everything.

Bobbi pulled her dreamy thoughts back to the present and rejoined Savon in the conversation. "I think your ideas are brilliant, but having you as a client is not. Things got messy before and affected how I work. And—"

"Okay . . . okay," he said, waving his hand. "I get it." Savon sighed. "I'm sorry for how I handled things and I promise it won't happen again. You accept my apology?"

"Yes. And I told you so last week. But your apology has nothing to do with us continuing to do business together."

"I guess I have to respect that. But you promise to think about it?" he said, smiling.

"Sure, I'll think about it," said Bobbi.

"Sooo . . . now that we've made up, can a brutha get a hug? What's up?" Savon flashed her a smile she couldn't deny.

"I don't want to, but yes." A smile spread slowly across Bobbi's face. "Don't hurt me again. Understood?" She pointed a scolding finger at him.

"Loud and clear." Savon grinned.

Bobbi left her seat and walked into Savon's outstretched arms. After a lingering hug, Bobbi pulled back first, but not before he kissed her cheek. She stepped back further and brushed the front of her clothes. Clearing her throat, she said, "I still need to consider the proposal, so I'll get back to you with an answer in a few days."

"Of course," he said. This wasn't the answer Savon wanted to hear, but it would do for now.

"Mister Turner. I hate to put you out, but I'm leaving shortly and need to get a few things done before I go." She and Nikki had a spa day planned and nothing would stop her from getting out of there on time.

"It doesn't sound like you hate putting me out," he chuckled.

Bobbi grabbed Savon by the hand and led him toward the door—an innocent gesture she hadn't expected to feel intimate. He left the office, walking past Ciara and out the glass door. Bobbi went back to her office and dropped her face in her hands. Why had she grabbed his hand? And that cheek kiss—she'd felt it all over. Even her body betrayed her.

A couple of days later, Savon called and invited her to hang out with him and a few friends on the Potomac River. He and his boys were renting a yacht and planning a couple's day out on the water next weekend. At first she said no, but when Savon resorted to begging, she gave in.

The day of the yacht excursion, Bobbi stood in the closet flipping through jeans and sweaters. She'd already changed clothes twice. What do you wear on a boat in April with a man who dissed you? Hmmm. Bobbi threw up her hands and put back on the jeans and fitted sweater she'd first tried on, and then went downstairs to wait for Savon.

The phone rang while she watered her plants in the family room.

"Hey, Lance. What's up?" she said.

"Hey. You wanna hang out today? Maybe we can go into DC and check out some museums or something."

"Aww. That would be cool, but I already have plans."

"Oh," said Lance. "Maybe another time."

The doorbell rang and Bobbi swallowed hard. "Uh . . . sure. I gotta go. I'll catch up with you next week." She hung up the phone and put the watering pot on the kitchen counter.

Bobbi went to the door, took a deep breath and opened it. Savon stepped inside and took Bobbi into his arms, squeezing her tight. His lips brushed against her ear.

"You ready?" he said.

"Sure," said Bobbi. But she didn't know whether to slap Savon for kissing her ear or pull off her clothes. The man was driving her bananas.

"Let's do it," he said, grabbing her hand.

"Wait a minute. I forgot something. I'll meet you at the car," she said.

Bobbi pulled her hand away and went back inside, closing the door behind her. She prayed that Savon would keep his gifted hands to himself today so she could manage her hormones.

But on the yacht, nothing changed. Savon held her hand or had some part of his body touching hers the entire time they sailed.

Whenever he was close enough, he would drape his arm over her shoulder or his leg would be touching hers if they were sitting together. The times they were out on the deck, he stood behind her with his body against hers. The sexual tension had her stomach in knots.

Besides them, five other couples were on the boat, but none were married. Bobbi and three of the ladies befriended each other and had a chance to chat while the guys were in another area smoking cigars. The other two were clearly party girls looking for a good time, which made Bobbi wonder why Savon had invited her.

At sundown, the lavish boat docked at the National Harbor, and both Savon and Bobbi were glad to be back on dry land. On the ride back to her house, they made plans for dinner at a pub with a live band not far from Bobbi's house. Savon dropped Bobbi off at home to freshen up, but before she got out the car, he leaned over and gently kissed her lips.

"I'll be back at eight," he said, looking into her eyes. "I'm gonna check into a hotel, get showered and changed, and then I'll be back."

"Okay." Bobbi smiled at Savon and got out of the car.

When she made it to her bedroom, she fell on the bed and screamed as loud as she could into a pillow. Savon was doing the most. She hadn't anticipated his lovey-dovey behavior today. All the touching and that kiss in the car had her on edge.

Bobbi took a bubble bath and put on the perfect little red dress. When Savon returned, he stepped inside and pulled Bobbi to him.

"You're so beautiful," he said.

"Thank you."

They stood in the foyer of her townhome, sharing a kiss that picked up where they'd left off back in January, before Monica had interrupted their lives.

Bobbi came up for air first and wiped at her red lipstick. She looked at Savon, wondering what this man was trying to do to her. Didn't he know she was weak for him?

"I guess you missed me while you were at the hotel, huh?" said Bobbi.

"Mmm hmm. Come back here." Savon pulled Bobbi back in and kissed her again.

Bobbi stepped back. "Pump your brakes. We need to go eat. So get yourself together and put that tongue back in your mouth." Bobbi took her fingers and closed his lips.

Savon burst out laughing. "Okay . . . I hear you."

Bobbi went to the kitchen and called for Savon. She met him with a napkin and wiped the traces of lipstick off of his mouth. "There," she said. "Now, let's go."

At the restaurant, Savon and Bobbi were seated at a table near the area where the band would play later. They ordered and settled in for a relaxing meal after a full day.

Bobbi looked thoughtfully across the table at Savon. There were things she wanted to ask him about the situation with Monica, but tonight wasn't the time. Then again, maybe she never would, because it might hurt too much to know. Bobbi let out a heavy sigh and smiled back at the man of her dreams.

By the time the band set up, Savon and Bobbi were finished with dinner. They spent the night dancing close and enjoying each other's company. Bobbi believed Savon's apology had been genuine and that he truly wanted to prove that his feelings for her hadn't changed.

After they left the restaurant, things got hot and heavy back at Bobbi's place. They were snuggled up on the sofa talking, and before long Savon's hands were all over her. Bobbi knew exactly where this scenario was headed. Yes, she'd forgiven Savon, and her hormones were raging right now, but he didn't deserve that part of her. So she played her part a few minutes longer, then kindly escorted him and his busy hands to the door. He would have to earn his way back into her bed. And long-stemmed roses with honey-dipped apologies weren't quite enough.

Chapter 19

When Bobbi got a call from Savon about spending time with him at his NYC apartment for the Memorial Day weekend, she got excited. New York had to be her favorite place on the planet and it happened to be most beautiful in spring. Bobbi longed for a change of pace, and welcomed a break from the office.

The morning of her trip, she called Savon to do a pulse check before taking the ride to see him. Although things were amicable between them, spending a weekend at his place made her nervous.

"Hey. I'm on my way," she said, standing on the platform at Union Station. "Are we still good?"

"Girl, get on the train," said Savon. He chuckled. "Hey . . . I can't wait to see you."

Bobbi tried, but couldn't hold back the smile in her voice. "Me too."

She boarded the train and took the four-hour ride from DC to Penn Station in Midtown Manhattan. Bobbi took out her laptop and went to the dining car to get some work done. Lil Dizzy had been causing trouble again, so she had plenty to do to occupy her time. However, thoughts of Savon kept creeping in. She wondered if their visit would be awkward. Would he be different in his own environment? And, how were they going to stay in the same house and not wind up in bed together? Bobbi shook her head knowingly. They needed a chaperone.

When she arrived in Manhattan and stepped out of the train station, Savon was parked at the corner in a black Porsche. He got out and put her bag in the trunk and they took off. When they arrived at his apartment, he parked in the underground garage and they took the elevator up to the twelfth floor. In the small, steel space, Savon bent down and kissed Bobbi and they got reacquainted. He missed everything about this woman: her fruity scent, being next to her body, and of course those lips.

Inside the apartment, Savon let go of her luggage and went for a deeper kiss. His hands were all over her. Bobbi moved a hand off of her butt and called a time-out.

"Whooa, horsey," she said, wiping at her lips. "Do I need to get a hotel for these two days?"

Savon grunted. "I missed you . . . that's all. Nah . . . you won't be getting a hotel room." He pulled her back to him and kissed her forehead, then led her to his master bedroom suite. "This is where you'll sleep," he said. "I'll be in one of the guest bedrooms."

Savon's phone rang, and he told Bobbi to take a tour of the apartment while he took the call. When he left the room, she rubbed her hands together, ready to inspect the place for hairpins, earrings, tampons—and anything else that would reveal what Savon had been up to.

Back in the living room, Bobbi loved the floor-to-ceiling windows and the skyline view of Manhattan. Every room had black furniture with either cherry wood or chrome accessories and smelled like fresh linen air spray. When she went into the kitchen and opened the cabinets, she giggled when she saw black dishes.

"What are you doing," said Savon, reaching around her waist from the back.

Bobbi jumped and turned to face him. "Don't scare me like that."

Savon chuckled. "I didn't mean to scare you. What do you want to do now?" he said, stroking her hair. "We're going out later, but we have time to do whatever you want."

"Can we go shopping? I wanna check out some stores on Fifth Avenue while I'm here." Bobbi had packed a couple of party dresses just in case, but she wanted to see if she could find something a tad sexier. She had to be on point in the fashion mecca.

"Sure," he said.

Savon took Bobbi to the stores of her choosing and paid the bill. Although Bobbi didn't need him to pick up her tabs, it delighted her to see him do it. She'd taken notice of his efforts to make up for the past, but this had exceeded anything she ever expected.

After shopping, they went to dinner in SoHo to one of Savon's favorite Mediterranean restaurants. By the time they got back to his place, it was nine-thirty. Savon followed Bobbi to the master suite and lay across the bed. He watched as she admired the things he'd purchased for her.

"Thanks again for buying these things," said Bobbi.

"No problem." He got up off the bed. "Get some rest. We need to leave for the club in two hours."

At midnight, they strolled into the club, hand in hand, and made their way to the VIP section. Savon introduced Bobbi to his friends—a few of whom she'd met last month on the yacht. Someone passed them champagne and Bobbi clinked glasses with Savon.

"To new beginnings," she said.

"Yeah . . . new beginnings." Savon threw his arm over her shoulder.

Bobbi stood next to him bobbing her head to the loud music, which vibrated in her chest. She'd stopped going to nightclubs about two years ago when she'd turned thirty, never wanting to feel like the old lady in the club. But tonight was a good break from the routine.

She snuggled closer to Savon, sipping her drink and looking around the crowded nightspot. When Bobbi caught the eyes of a few haters sitting on a couch a few feet away, she winked at them and they frowned and whispered to each other.

"You okay?" said Savon. His breath was warm against her ear. She smiled. "I'm good."

So far, Savon had been on his best behavior—he'd been the perfect gentleman. And that made Bobbi happy. With that in mind, she made a pact with her self to dismiss every doubt and thoughts of regret for allowing him back into her life. She wanted to enjoy the weekend and let this man treat her like she deserved.

The next morning, Bobbi woke up to the smell of bacon and cinnamon. She stretched and called for Savon. When he said he'd be there in a minute, she got up and padded across the cool hardwood floor to the bathroom. Savon still wasn't there when she came out, so she went to him in the kitchen. She walked up behind him, putting her arms around his waist.

"Mmmm. Smells good." She moved to his side.

Savon looked down at her and she stood on tiptoe to kiss him.

"I told you I was coming," he said. "Get back in bed. I'm bringing you breakfast."

"Okay. But you need to stop spoiling me, unless you want a permanent houseguest." She smiled up at him. "I'm serious."

"Go get in the bed," said Savon. He smacked her butt when she turned to leave.

Bobbi got back in bed and Savon came in shortly afterward, carrying a tray with bacon and eggs and French toast. He joined her under the covers and they ate and talked about last night.

The club had been okay, but they were ready to leave an hour after they'd arrived. So they left the club and ditched the car at Savon's apartment and caught a cab to *B.B. King Blues Club & Grill.* They'd listened to R&B and talked for hours.

Bobbi rubbed her belly, chewing the last bite of bacon.

"That was delicious. I didn't know you could cook."

"Yeah. I got mad skills in the kitchen," said Savon, with his chest pumped up.

"Well . . . my compliments to the chef."

Bobbi leaned over and kissed him, and then gathered their dishes on the tray and carried them into the kitchen. When she returned to the bedroom, Savon was gone. She found him in another bedroom, stretched out on the bed with his hands behind his head, watching TV and listening to commentary from former athletes. Bobbi sat next to him and he pulled her close.

The sportscasters talked about the Washington Warriors and mentioned how well Savon had performed during the regular season last year. They said that his speed as a wide receiver had increased over the past two seasons with the Condors and now with the Warriors, making him one of the players to watch this year.

Bobbi teased Savon. "Okay . . . I see you, Mister one-to-watch."

Savon chuckled. "Just remember that," he said, then he rolled her on top of him.

"I told you I don't really follow football," said Bobbi. "I see the sports highlights on the news and that's enough for me to know if Washington won or not. And that's really the whole point, right—to know which team won?"

Shaking his head, Savon said, "No, love, it's not enough. Your man is in the NFL, so I need you to know what I do for a living."

"My man? Says who? I don't remember agreeing to that."

Savon grinned. "You will," he said, looking into her eyes. "What do you wanna do today?"

Bobbi ignored his comment and repositioned herself to lie beside him. "Let's go for a ride and just hang out. Treat me like a tourist and show me New York."

"Okay." Savon rolled her back on top of him and they talked for a long while before leaving his apartment.

That night, when they returned from sightseeing and more shopping, Bobbi went to pack her bags for her trip back to DC tomorrow afternoon. She had new sandals, sundresses, and a few other pieces to try and squeeze into the one suitcase she'd brought. While packing, Savon entered the room and sat in the black leather recliner next to the bed.

"Can you stay a couple more days?" he said.

"Huh?" Bobbi's eyes bucked and she sat down on the bed.

"I'm not ready for you to leave. Can you stay until Tuesday?" Savon reached for her hand.

She met the questioning look in his eyes with one of her own. "Ah . . . maybe. I need to check my calendar."

Bobbi pulled out her phone to scroll through her calendar. Besides juggling the work she had to do with Lil Dizzy, she could literally work from anywhere with her laptop and phone. She told Savon that she needed to make a few calls, and he excused himself.

Bobbi turned on her laptop and video chatted with Ciara as they reviewed her schedule for the week.

They talked through the appointments on Bobbi's calendar for Tuesday and Wednesday and moved some things around. Bobbi told Ciara to send out emails to reschedule a few meetings and then ended the call. After that, she called and canceled her train reservation, and went to let Savon know that she could stay.

"So," she said, smiling up at him. "I can stay, but I need to get back home early Wednesday."

A smile spread across his lips and he tackled her onto the sofa. "I've got plans for you."

Bobbi bit her bottom lip. "What do you mean?" she said, her voice shaky.

"Don't worry. It's nothing you can't handle."

Savon told Bobbi that she could ride back to DC with him, since he had to be back for offseason workouts on Wednesday anyways. She told him okay then pushed him off of her, and he fell to the floor.

"I'll get you back later," he said to her retreating back, as she ran off.

Bobbi showered and went back to the living room where she found Savon in black boxers sprawled out on the sectional watching television. He told her to come lie next to him, and she hesitated.

"Uhm . . . I don't want to." A nervous grin escaped her lips.

"Stop being a chicken," he said. "I don't bite."

Bobbi chuckled. "Yes, you do."

He laughed. "I promise not to bother you. We can watch a movie."

Bobbi shook a finger at him. "Okay, now. But I'm serious," she said. Then she settled down on the sofa next to him and they cuddled.

Sometime later, in the wee hours of the morning, Savon turned and rested his muscular leg overtop Bobbi's thighs, waking her up. She rubbed her eyes and read the glowing green numbers on the cable box.

She poked Savon in the arm and he didn't move, so she pushed his leg off of her and tiptoed to the master bedroom to safety, and fell back asleep.

A couple of hours later, a cool draft assaulted Savon's bare skin and he stirred, reaching for Bobbi. Realizing that she'd gone, he sat up and rubbed a hand over his manhood. He wanted Bobbi so bad. The whole waiting thing could be admirable, he guessed, but he couldn't shake the visions of him ravishing her body.

Savon got up and went to his master suite. He would deal with whatever consequences he had to face after the fact. Right now, he wanted to make love to his woman. When he entered the bedroom, he found Bobbi asleep on her side. He threw back the bed sheet and put his mouth where he wanted it. When Bobbi stirred, he shifted her hips so that she lay on her back.

Disoriented, Bobbi felt Savon's arms around her legs, and then the distinct sense of pleasure down below. She opened her eyes and reached for his head.

"Savon, what are you doing?"

He didn't answer.

Bobbi's head fell back on the pillow. She didn't stop him—she didn't want to. Her body responded to his appetite and she released in no time. Then Savon came to lie on top of her.

"I want you," he said.

From there he entered her, and they both gave in to passion. Until well after sunrise, Savon and Bobbi explored this familiar place in their new relationship.

All day Monday and Tuesday, little else went down outside of the bedroom. They managed to go out for dinner Monday night and Bobbi pulled away from Savon a few hours on Tuesday to handle work stuff, but other than that, they couldn't keep their hands off of each other.

Early Wednesday morning, Savon and Bobbi loaded up his Escalade and drove to DC. Both were at a new level of thinking about the other. For Savon, there couldn't be a more perfect woman for him than Bobbi. Even as they traveled together right now, he could see himself being with her for the foreseeable future. And as for Bobbi, Savon had proven to be a gentleman and a gentle man, and she appreciated his efforts to make things right with her again.

Chapter 20

Back at work, scenes from the last four days played like a video in Bobbi's head. So much had happened. She couldn't focus on work no matter how hard she tried. So, she pushed the stack of folders to the side and called Nikki.

"Your girlfriend has been a slut puppy all weekend," Bobbi blurted when Nikki answered.

"Oh, goodness. What did you do?" said Nikki, taking her hand from the nail tech to position the phone on her shoulder.

"Girl, I'm too shame to tell you. Let's just say, Savon rocked my entire world."

"What? You gave him some? Homeboy would've had to buy me two Gucci bags with the matching shoes and belts, and a Bentley before he could even sniff my goodies again. I'm just sayin'."

"Well, he practically did—just not the Bentley." Bobbi laughed. "Hey, can you come over tonight?"

"Uhm . . . yeah," said Nikki, switching the phone to the other shoulder. "I have a meeting on your side of town in the morning . . . I should spend the night."

"You should," said Bobbi. "I'll pick up dinner and see you around seven."

"Bet. See you later," said Nikki.

Next, Bobbi returned Lance's call. He'd left a couple of messages since the last time he'd asked her to hang out. But Lance didn't answer, so she left him a message and got back to work.

On her way home, Bobbi picked up baked chicken with brown rice and veggies. Lance called as she pulled into the driveway.

"Hello, stranger," said Bobbi.

"I'm not a stranger, Bobbi. But you sure are a busy woman. You've been out of town?" Lance didn't like that Bobbi hadn't been in the office the last few times he stopped by. And he knew she wasn't working from home because Ciara would have told him so.

"Uh . . . yeah. I went to visit a friend." Bobbi frowned. "What's up," she said, washing her hands and taking the food out of the bag.

"I wanted to make sure you're okay, and to see if you want to link up and do something—anything," Lance said.

"Sure. But can we talk about it later? I just walked in the door and I'm pooped."

"No problem. Goodnight." Lance clenched his teeth as he hung up the phone. He'd thought Bobbi enjoyed his company. But she'd made it clear tonight—she wasn't interested in getting to know him.

Soon after, Nikki knocked on the door and Bobbi went to let her in. They had a lot to talk about. Even though Nikki had been with her through the tears and heartbreak with Savon, she hoped Nikki would be happy for her and give Savon a second chance just as she had.

The two friends ate dinner and then moved to the family room with dessert. Nikki had brought over carrot cake for them to indulge in while they shared the juicy drama in their lives. Bobbi went first, talking about Savon and how he wanted them to think about a future together.

"You mean after all the cockamamie madness he put you through, you believe you can trust him again?" said Nikki.

Bobbi looked away. Nikki had a point, but she had forgiven Savon and that meant they were starting over with a clean slate. "I know what he did was wrong. And I hated his guts for it. But I've forgiven him, so I'm trying to stay positive and put the past behind me."

"Yeah, but it wasn't that long ago, boo. How do you know Monica is out of the picture for real? Remember what happened the last time she was supposedly out of his life."

Bobbi picked at a pecan in the frosting on her cake. She didn't have an answer for Nikki. Everything she'd said was true. But Bobbi wanted to be with Savon and she couldn't explain why.

Nikki realized her comments had dampened Bobbi's mood so she added, "Well . . . at least he's trying to make things right—so he gets points for that. But he'll come up missing if he hurts you again." She nudged Bobbi. "I'm serious. And if that clown Monica comes back, we'll double-team her butt. Ya heard me?"

Bobbi smiled at her ride-or-die friend. "You can best believe I'm not dealing with Monica again or any bad behavior from Savon. On my life, I'm not doing it."

Nikki put down the cake plate and pulled the blanket up over her legs. "Enough about Savon. What's up with Lance? I really like him."

"Girl, Lance is just a little too clingy for me. He's been trying to hang out, but I haven't had time. And he actually tried to call me out on it. Can you believe that?" said Bobbi.

"Yeah, I can. I think he likes you. And the man is fine if I have to say so myself."

"Don't say that." Bobbi frowned. "Yeah, he's fine and cool and all that, but he has a kid and I'm not about that life right now. I knew this was going to happen and that's why I tried to keep it cordial in the first place. Huuhhh!"

"Well . . . he's a big boy—so don't worry about him. I'm just saying he's a good guy."

The two friends talked about everything they could think of including Nikki and Todd's plans to meet each other's families— things were getting serious. They talked about being in love and Bobbi pulled out the letter from Sister Ruth. Although Nikki had heard about Bobbi's counseling session and the letter months ago, this was the first time they'd discussed what love really looked like in their lives. Hours later, they fell off to sleep with the television on and the love letter lying between them on the sofa.

———◆———

Savon and Bobbi connected every day by phone or text after she returned from New York. Bobbi even made a trip back to Manhattan with Savon after minicamp in mid-June. She stayed with him for a week, using the time to strategize about his brand and the direction he wanted his career to go. Even though they mixed business and pleasure again, Bobbi felt secure in their personal dealings, and confident that she could continue to help his career at the same time.

During preseason training camp, the media couldn't get enough of Savon. This only helped Bobbi's pitch to top brands in the entertainment and sports industries for endorsement deals. As the sports commentators had said months ago, Savon was indeed "the one to watch."

By the time the Warriors played their first game of the season, Savon had an Under Armour deal and a high-end, used car dealership commercial locked in. Soon, the money would be rolling in for both of them and they'd just gotten started. Bobbi had big plans and even bigger business deals for her man as the season progressed.

Meanwhile, one Saturday morning in September, Bobbi struggled to pull herself together. Savon would be there soon for their pregame meal and a movie. She flushed the toilet and rinsed her mouth. That was her second time throwing up this week.

Bobbi went downstairs to check on lunch. She'd cooked steak and a baked potato for Savon—his ritual meal the day before a game—and made salmon for herself. With their business schedules, weekends were the only days they could spend quality time since the season started.

Savon knocked on the door and she let him in.

"Hey, bae," said Bobbi, greeting him with a kiss.

"What's up?" He smacked her on the butt when she turned to walk away.

In the kitchen they had lunch and talked about the commercial deal she secured for him and the upcoming videotaping. Savon was excited and nervous. He rehearsed his lines so much that Bobbi had threatened to tell the producer they weren't interested anymore if he didn't give it a rest.

Later that evening, they sat on the sofa watching a movie and Savon held Bobbi close. Suddenly, she pushed out of his arms and ran to the bathroom. But she didn't make it in time. Most of the salmon and asparagus she'd had for lunch, splattered over the bathroom floor.

Savon followed her. "Are you okay, love?" he said.

"I really don't know, babe. I'm exhausted—and I keep throwing up. Maybe I have the flu or a stomach virus or something."

Savon helped Bobbi clean the last of the mess off the floor. Then watched as she sat on the commode, with her face in her hands.

"Come on. Let me put you in bed," he said, grabbing her hand.

Savon held Bobbi around the waist and walked her to the bedroom. He pulled back the covers and tucked her in. Then he went to get a wet washcloth.

"What's that for?" she said.

"It's for your head. I see them do it on TV all the time."

Bobbi snatched the washcloth and threw it at him. "You're crazy, babe." She chuckled. Her man could be so silly at times.

Before long, she drifted off to sleep with Savon at her side.

Early the next morning, Bobbi gave Savon her usual game-day pep talk and kissed him. "Now go out there and win," she said.

Savon winked at his woman and smiled. "Okay," he said, wondering why she always said that, knowing he played with a team.

After Savon left, Bobbi tried to get her own head in the game. She wanted to go, but the thought of getting NFL girlfriend-cute with four-inch heels, glammed up hair and makeup and the perfect outfit, made her want to barf again. She couldn't do that today.

Bobbi texted Savon around noon and told him that she was on her way to the urgent care clinic, but not to worry—she would talk to him after the game. An hour later, Bobbi sat on the exam table flipping through a magazine. She'd been triaged and so far everything seemed normal. But they were waiting for lab results for the flu test she'd been given half an hour ago.

An Asian doctor entered the room, greeted Bobbi and then washed his hands. He looked over her chart nodding his head, then smiled at Bobbi.

"Congratulations, Miss Farqua. You're pregnant."

"Pregnant? What?!"

"Yes. Pregnant," the doctor repeated. "You should make an appointment with your OBGYN right away to start prenatal care. Oh . . . and your flu results are negative. The nurse will be in with discharge instructions." He shook her hand and left.

Bobbi managed a strained smiled and nodded her head. Once the nurse came in and told her what to do, she couldn't get out of there quick enough.

She drove home with mixed emotions. This news had blind-sided her—it had not occurred to her at all that she could be pregnant. When Bobbi had arrived at the clinic and the nurse took her vital signs, she'd been asked if she could be pregnant, and of course she'd said no. Every time a woman goes to the doctor she's asked that question, no matter the ailment. Somehow, in the medical field, everything gets connected to the uterus.

Stopped at a red light a few blocks from her house, Bobbi decided to do her own pregnancy test. The doctor could be wrong. She and Savon almost always used protection. There were only a handful of times that the condom came off or broke and, once they realized it, they took care of the problem. Maybe not right away, but they did handle it. Plus, she'd had her period last month.

When the light changed, Bobbi dashed over to the drug store and picked up three different brands of pregnancy tests. If even one test were negative, she would be relieved. Although she wanted a family some day, she didn't want it to happen like this. She and Savon did business deals, not diapers.

At home, Bobbi took all three tests out of the bag and went to the bathroom. She sat on the toilet and with shaky hands, took the white testing sticks out of the boxes and held each one under the flow of her urine. Then she laid them on the sink and waited. Within seconds, a solid pink line formed on two of the tests, but nothing happened with the third. Bobbi's foot tapped and she prayed, hoping at least one thing would be different than the news she'd received today. But the last test revealed her pregnancy too, just before nausea overtook her and she vomited.

An hour later, curled up on the family room sofa in front of the tube, Bobbi watched Savon catch a long pass with one hand, over two defenders. "Do it, boo!" she said, leaning up on her elbow. He even got a few steps in before being tackled. In the fourth quarter and final seconds of the game, the Warriors were down by three. Savon caught another long pass and Bobbi sat up, cheering him on as he ran thirty yards into the end zone, winning the game for the Warriors.

"Whoop, whoop! That's my baby!" she said, doing the cabbage patch. She had told him to win.

Chapter 21

"Bae, did you see? We won!"

Bobbi grinned. "I did see you, bae. I was cheering the whole time." Bobbi sat up on the sofa and put the phone on speaker.

"Can you come over tonight? I want to see you," said Savon.

Bobbi didn't want to go anywhere. Taking a nap once the game went off had helped, but she was still tired. Nonetheless, she couldn't miss celebrating this victory with her man.

"Okay. I'll be there by eight-thirty," Bobbi said.

"Alright, love . . . drive safe."

On the way to see Savon, Bobbi could hear the urgent care doctor's announcement ringing in her ear. *Congratulations. You're pregnant!* How was she going to tell Savon? What would he say? How would this change their relationship?

When Bobbi arrived at Savon's house, she stuck her key in the door and went inside. Savon had guests—loud guests—who were all talking about the big win and enjoying themselves. He made his way over and greeted Bobbi, holding her close for a moment, talking about the game, and she told him how proud she was.

"See, babe? I told you to win and you did." She kissed him.

"I know. You're my good luck piece."

Savon held Bobbi at the waist as they walked into the great room where all the guests were hanging out, and she joined the conversation. Even though she still didn't know much football lingo, she held her own. In an attempt to coach her before the season started, Savon had told Bobbi that all she needed to remember was offense, defense, and touchdown. He'd said that if she knew who had the ball, she would know how to cheer—and every time the Warriors had the ball and brought it to the end zone, they scored.

Bobbi watched Savon interact with his friends and teammates. His animated replay of his performance on the field tickled her. But the smile plastered on his face is what warmed Bobbi's heart. She only hoped that he would be just as thrilled about the pregnancy.

The next morning, Bobbi lay in Savon's arms, anxious to share her news. Having a baby wasn't a topic they'd discussed before so she had no idea how he would respond. Heck, she didn't even know how to feel about it, and she was the one barfing every day with four positive tests.

Bobbi crawled out of bed and went to the bathroom. She talked to herself in the mirror, practicing the different ways to initiate the conversation with Savon. But that had only made matters worse. Now she had sweaty palms and a dry mouth. Bobbi brushed her teeth and went back to bed. An hour later Savon woke up.

"Good morning, love," he said.

Bobbi stretched and smiled at her man. "Good morning."

"You feeling better today?" he said, rubbing her belly. "What did the doctor say?"

Bobbi placed her hand on top of his, relishing the strength of his warm fingers against her skin. It was show time. "Ummh . . . well . . . the doctor said I'm, uhhh . . . I'm preggers."

"What?" Savon sat up.

"Pregnant. The doctor said I'm pregnant." Bobbi sat up too.

"What do you mean you're pregnant?"

"That's what's wrong with me. I mean—that's what's going on with me."

"That's just one test, though," said Savon. "I've heard of false positives—"

"Me too. So I went to the CVS and bought three tests, and they all came back positive too."

Savon's jaw clenched and he looked away. Then he went to the bathroom without a word.

Bobbi assumed he didn't like the news. Otherwise, he would have done more than ask questions about the validity of the test. When he came back in the room, she questioned him.

"So, how do you feel about the baby?" she said.

"I don't want kids," he said. His dislike for the topic etched in his face.

"Since when?" Bobbi felt bile rise in her throat. "You never told me that."

"We never talked about it. And you never told me you wanted kids." Savon sat next to her. "You're chasing your career and I'm doing the same thing. I didn't know you wanted kids."

"I mean, I haven't spent a lot of time thinking about it, but I'm not against it." Bobbi's bottom lip quivered as the weight of his words became clear. But she had to ask one more time. "So, what are you saying?"

"I'm saying that I don't want kids." He looked her square in the eyes.

Bobbi threw back the covers and stormed out of the room. She needed to calm down before she lost it on his behind. What did he mean by, he didn't want kids? She was pregnant now!

When she came back, Savon watched her get dressed. This time, she didn't say anything. Before she left the house, Savon stopped her and lifted her chin to look into her eyes.

"We'll figure it out," he said. "Please don't be upset with me, okay?"

Bobbi gave him the faintest inkling of a smile and said, "I'll talk to you later," and then she left.

It took Bobbi longer than usual to get ready for work. The finality of Savon's words had surprised her, and had even weighted her down with sadness. She loved Savon and wanted to be with him. He had proven to be a kind and loving man who wanted to do right by people—and that's what she liked so much about him. So this didn't make sense.

Bobbi sighed as she pulled on her panty hose and slid her feet into a pair of brown pumps. She walked across the room and gathered some folders off the bed and put them in her briefcase.

Once she had everything together, Bobbi sat down in the chair next to the bed. She needed to clear her head before going into the office. She pulled up pictures of Savon in her phone and smiled at his handsome face, remembering that he wasn't perfect and neither was she. They made their love work, and this would work out, too. Savon would have a change of heart once he had time to process things—she just knew it. They had love and a solid relationship. Those reasons alone should cause his heart to change about the baby.

Looking down at her belly, Bobbi gently rubbed where she thought the baby might be.

"Hi, there little person. What a surprise to learn about you. Mommy and daddy are trying to figure things out for you." Bobbi closed her eyes and prayed that everything would work out.

———◦——

At one o'clock, Bobbi arrived at the office to find Lil Dizzy and his management team in the waiting area. They didn't have an appointment, and Ciara hadn't called to let her know they were even there. Bobbi sighed. She didn't need any more surprises today.

She looked to Ciara for a clue, but she shrugged her shoulders. So Bobbi took a calming breath and walked over to the group.

"Hi, guys. Hey, Dizzy," said Bobbi. She touched Dizzy's shoulder and smiled at the teenager. "What's going on? Did I miss something?"

Dizzy's manager stood up to greet her. "Bobbi, we need your help," he said, with wrinkles creasing his forehead. "Some things happened over the weekend that got out of control and we need you to make it go away. You know—work your magic."

Bobbi looked between the manager and the other four men— their faces were riddled with concern. But Dizzy looked normal with a pair of headphones covering his ears, his head bobbing up and down.

"Ciara, please show these gentleman to the conference room," said Bobbi.

Ciara got up and offered them water and then led the men toward the back of the suite.

But Bobbi held Dizzy back in the waiting area. "What happened?" she said.

Dizzy uncovered one of his ears. "Man . . . they overreacted. I'm cool," he said, then covered his ear again.

Of course Bobbi knew there had to be more to the story, and she also knew that if Dizzy sat in the conference room with them, solving the problem would be impossible because of his nonchalant attitude.

So Bobbi called Lance, and asked if Dizzy could hang out with him for an hour. To her surprise, Lance didn't hesitate. He told her to bring him to the office.

When Bobbi and Dizzy arrived in Lance's suite, she introduced Lil Dizzy, and Lance pointed toward his office and told him to go and have a seat. Bobbi looked sideways at Lance. His delivery seemed rough and even mean considering he and Dizzy were meeting for the first time.

"Are you okay," said Bobbi, touching Lance's arm.

"I'm fine," he said, his eyes piercing to her soul.

"Oh. Uhmm . . . are you sure it's okay for Dizzy to stay. He can sit in my office and listen to music if this is a bad time." Lance seemed irritated, and Bobbi had a good idea why.

"I told you to bring him, and I meant it. Just call when you want him to come back."

Bobbi smiled. "I really appreciate your help with this." She grabbed his arm and moved in closer. "Walk with me to the elevator, please." Her hand slid down his wrist and she locked her fingers with his as they left his office. "Why are you being mean today? It doesn't suit you?"

Lance pressed the elevator button and looked at her. "What do you mean?"

"You know exactly what I mean." Her eyebrow raised, Bobbi gave him a knowing look. "Be nice."

Lance chuckled. "I got you."

When the elevator opened, Bobbi hugged Lance and he loosened up with her touch. On the ride to her floor, Bobbi realized that she and Lance hadn't hung out since April, and here it was September. They'd only seen each other in passing at work. And every time he'd called, she'd been too busy to talk or she already had plans. Her priorities had shifted away from Lance just as their friendship began.

Back in her office, Bobbi learned the reason for the management team's visit. The young rapper had been at a nightclub over the weekend, breaking the law and talking trash to some other rapper's girlfriend. A fight between the two broke out later that night at an after-hours joint, and Dizzy had been yanked up and taken away by his camp before the police arrived. But the rapper he'd disrespected declared war. To think, at 16 years old, having to look over his shoulder every day, wondering if he would be jumped or worse. Dizzy had to make some changes, and fast.

His team had brought him to Bobbi's office because they were at their wits end with the young man. They wanted her to talk to Dizzy and also see if she could run some interference with the other rapper's camp to call a truce. Although this wasn't a PR issue per se, the management team knew that Bobbi cared for the boy and wanted to see him win.

Three hours later, Bobbi called Lance to bring Lil Dizzy back, but they were out shooting hoops. Thirty minutes after the call, they entered the conference room. Dizzy gave Lance a fist pound and blew it up before taking a seat at the table. He and Lance laughed at the gesture, while Bobbi and the management team gazed at each other in disbelief. From the looks on everyone's faces, they wanted to know what had happened in the last few hours to turn the little demon spawn into a playful teen.

No one asked Lance to leave, so he stayed while Bobbi and the group talked to Dizzy about his behavior and the deal Bobbi had made working through the other rapper's publicist.

Before the meeting ended, Lance asked if he could call Dizzy and hang out with him every now and then. Everyone at the table looked at each other and then at Dizzy, who still had a big smile on his face.

Dizzy's manager spoke up. "We'll talk with his grandmother and get back to you."

Lance gave the manager a business card and said, "I look forward to hearing from you and Dizzy's grandmother."

After everyone left, Bobbi tidied the conference room and then she and Lance moved to her office. They talked about Dizzy and the events of the day. She still couldn't believe how different Dizzy seemed after hanging out with Lance for only a few hours.

Bobbi's phone rang and she held up a finger toward Lance.

"Hello," she said.

"Hey, beautiful," said Savon. "What are you doing?"

"Still at work."

"We need to talk," he said. "I'm coming over tonight. What time will you be home?"

"By eight."

"Okay. And I'll bring dinner," said Savon.

"Okay. Bye."

Lance stood up to leave when Bobbi got off the phone. "I'll talk to you later," he said. Although he'd accepted that Bobbi had a man, he didn't want the relationship rubbed in his face.

"Okay," said Bobbi, standing to walk him out. "Thank you so much for the magic you worked with Dizzy today. I wouldn't have believed it if I didn't see it myself." She smiled.

"He's a cool young man—it was my pleasure. We'll be hanging out again real soon," said Lance.

Bobbi hugged Lance before he walked out of the suite, ignoring the obvious change in his demeanor after her phone call. His body had stiffened once again but she embraced him anyway. Lance had to learn his place in her life. He had become a trusted friend, but that was it.

Bobbi left the office at seven, wiped out from the long, taxing day. But besides Dizzy's miraculous attitude change being the peek of her day, she counted it a wonderful joy that Ciara had shared the cure for nausea, which had settled her stomach all day: plain kettle chips and ginger ale.

Chapter 22

Savon had dinner on the table when Bobbi walked through the door. She went to the kitchen to wash her hands and he walked up behind her and kissed her neck.

"How was your day, babe?" he said.

"Crazy." She turned to face him and kissed his lips. "I'm just glad it's over." She looked into his eyes and smiled, not knowing what to expect, but hoping for the best. "And how was your day?"

Savon took her face in his hands and kissed her gently on the lips. "It was cool. I'm getting ready for the Eagles game this weekend in Philly," he said. "But come on—let's eat."

They sat down and had their meal, enjoying each other's company while avoiding the real topic at hand. But the pleasantries were getting the best of Bobbi. She sipped her water and pushed the dinner plate away. Savon had some explaining to do after the hurtful things he'd said to here this morning.

"Let's talk about this pregnancy," said Bobbi. "That's why you're here, right? And I'm glad you came, because we really do need to figure this out."

Savon sighed and reached for Bobbi's hand. "I don't know what else to say. I love you, but I'm not going to change my mind about having kids, and I need you to respect that."

"What do you mean, respect that? I'm pregnant with your child." She put his hand on her belly. "Your baby is already inside of me. Do you get that?"

Savon snatched his hand back and jumped up from the table. He mumbled under his breath saying, "How did you get pregnant, anyway?"

"Get out! I heard what you said." Bobbi stood up. "What the heck do you mean, how did I get pregnant? Get out of my house!" She stomped toward the door with him on her heels.

"We still need to talk about this," said Savon. "We need to talk about you having an abortion." There. He had finally said the word. His plan tonight had been to convince Bobbi that he wasn't an evil, heartless guy who didn't care about her. Things were going well between them, even better than he'd imagined and he wanted the momentum to continue. A baby would only get in their way. And besides, him not wanting kids was a decision he'd made as a teenager. He didn't want the responsibility of fatherhood—ever.

Bobbi stood at the door, holding it open while she held back tears. "I can't believe you want me to have an abortion." The first tear fell. "How could you?" She dropped her head, and the floodgates opened.

Savon reached out his hand to console her, but then pulled it back not wanting to confuse Bobbi about his position on the matter. "I'll call you later," he said, and left.

Bobbi locked the door and went to her bedroom. In front of the full-length mirror, she rubbed her belly as the tears flowed. What was she going to do? Did she want to raise a child on her own? She didn't know the first thing about kids and parenting. But she did know that it would change her life forever.

After cleaning the kitchen, Bobbi got in bed. She wanted to call Nikki, but Nikki would make her feel foolish about being with Savon in the first place. And she didn't dare tell her mother and disappoint her. It would be humiliating and shameful to tell anyone that Savon flat-out didn't want the baby they'd made together.

Bobbi wiped at tears. She'd been wise in business, taking pride in knowing her clients before doing business with them, and yet she hadn't bothered to apply that same basic practice to her personal life. That had been her problem with men all along. She'd trusted them too soon, paying more attention to their words than their character.

Bobbi got out of bed and dropped to her knees to pray.

Father in heaven, I'm so hurt. Too hurt to fight—too hurt to be angry. I don't know what to do about the baby. At this point, I don't care what Savon thinks. Now I know that he doesn't care about me anyway. I just don't know if I'm ready to take care of another life by myself. God . . . please help me. Amen.

—————◦———————

On the drive home from the gynecologist, Bobbi's eyes brimmed with tears. She was six weeks pregnant. Shaking her head, she felt so alone. Whatever decision she made from this point would be solely on her, and she didn't like that.

Why did Savon get to skirt his responsibility, but she had to woman-up and handle business? Nonetheless, there had to be a way to reason with him. He had to be more humane than he'd shown her this week. Perhaps she needed to be patient with him and try a different approach.

With her mind made up, Bobbi pulled into a shopping center parking lot to call Savon. Once he realized how far along she was, the baby would become real to him.

"What's up," he said.

"I just came from the doctor. I'm six weeks."

"Okay. So what are you going to do about it?"

"Listen, Savon. I heard you when you said you don't want kids. And I understand this wasn't part of the game plan—it wasn't for me either—but I'm still pregnant." Bobbi spoke in her sweet, therapeutic voice. "So maybe we can talk about this with an open mind. I'm willing to if you are."

"No," he said, throwing clothes in his suitcase for his trip to Philly. "You know how I feel about you, but I don't want kids. I should have the right to say whether you bring a baby into the world from my seed."

"So you don't care that your baby is already growing inside of me?" Bobbi's face turned sour, wondering how he could be so harsh toward her.

"I'm not doing this with you, Bobbi. You need to get an abortion. You can come by and pick up the money or I'll bring it to you. But you need to take care of this and stop messing around."

"You are such a jerk!" she yelled into the phone. "All you care about is yourself!"

"And to think . . . I left Monica for you," Savon blurted. "At least she respected my decision not to have kids. But you—"

Bobbi cut him off. "How dare you bring up her name to me! I'm done! Lose my number and find someone else to represent you!" Bobbi hung up and burst into tears. Monica could have his two-bit, self-centered, hind-parts.

Bobbi sat in the waiting room of a women's clinic a few days later. She realized that something had to be done, and soon. After that last conversation with Savon, she'd had an epiphany. The whole relationship had been a lie. The way he treated her now was no different than he had back in January. Under pressure, he always cracked when it came to her. He had proven to be a coward time and again. As long as the relationship served his needs, they were good. But if the unexpected happened, he couldn't deal with it.

Folding her arms, Bobbi glanced around the waiting room, embarrassed that she would even be in this predicament. She needed someone who loved her to be in her corner right now. Although she didn't want to hear Nikki say I-told-you-so, she'd take her chances. So Bobbi stepped out of the waiting area, pushing through her shame, and called her best friend. Nikki's voicemail came on, and Bobbi left a message for her to call back—that it was urgent.

"Bobbi Farqua?" said the nurse who entered the waiting area with a clipboard.

"Hi. I'm Bobbi."

Bobbi followed the nurse into an exam room, where a specimen cup was handed to her along with instructions for collection. Once the lab results where back, a doctor entered the room and told Bobbi that she was about six or seven weeks pregnant. Bobbi nodded and swallowed hard.

Driving home, Bobbi couldn't help but think that no one she loved even knew what she'd been going through. It had been the loneliest time of her life. The doctor had given her three pills to insert into her vagina and told her that this would induce bleeding and thereby terminate the pregnancy.

Parked in her garage, tears wet Bobbi's cheeks as she stared at the brown pill bottle. Her sadness turned into sobs as she gave her pain a voice. How could she do it? Who was she to end a life? No one would win with this decision. Not her. Not Savon. Not least of all, their child.

After some time, Bobbi pulled herself together and went inside. In her bedroom, she took the pill bottle from her purse, unscrewed the cap, and shook the pills into her hand. She read the instructions again and lay on her back.

"I'm so sorry, little angel. Mommy is so sorry." Bobbi choked up. "God will take care of you. I'll see you in heaven."

The following day, the cramps started and Bobbi grieved her loss alone. She grieved the loss of her never-to-be-born child, the loss of her own innocence in the matter, and the loss of love she thought she had with Savon.

Chapter 23

Bobbi reached for her phone on the nightstand and turned it on. Last night she remembered that Nikki was in Jamaica with Todd for the week. So she'd turned off her phone to avoid any other callers. Now she had ten missed calls from Nikki and five voice messages. The last message she listened to said for her to expect a visit from Lance to check on her. *Great.*

Bobbi wasn't at all happy to hear that Nikki would be sending Lance on her behalf. Right now, she was a total mess—in her head and in appearance. Lance would pick up on her negative energy for sure, even if she tried to play it off.

She looked out the window then made her bed and went to freshen up. Applying a little eyeliner and mascara would distract from the puffy circles under her eyes. She pulled her hair in a high bun and went downstairs to wait for Lance.

With Nikki missing in action, Bobbi still needed someone to talk to for support. She pulled up Sister Ruth's name in her contact list and placed the call. Ruth didn't answer, so Bobbi left a message. It had been months since the two had chatted. At church, they would speak in passing, but Bobbi kept her distance because Ruth liked to get deep and Bobbi didn't always want to deal with that. But now she found herself desperate for the older woman's encouragement and comforting words.

Lance arrived within the hour and Bobbi went to answer the door.

"Hi, Lance. Come in," she said, welcoming him into her home for the first time.

"Hey. Is everything okay?" Lance gave her the once-over elevator eyes from head to toe. He guessed she looked okay, aside from the puffy eyes and ponytail, which he'd never seen her wear before.

"Yes, I'm fine." Bobbi watched Lance pull out his phone and make a call. He told the person on the other end that she was okay and everything was intact.

"Uhhh . . . is that Nikki?" said Bobbi. "Why are you talking about me like I'm not standing here?" She sucked her teeth and took the phone from him.

Lance followed Bobbi to the kitchen while she talked to Nikki. Bobbi told Nikki that she'd had a terrible disagreement with Savon and they'd broken up so she'd wanted to vent, but things were better now.

"Are you okay, though?" said Nikki. This was only the second day of her vacation, but she would come back tomorrow if Bobbi needed her.

"Yeah, I'm good. Forget I called. Really, I'm okay."

Lance tapped Bobbi on the shoulder and she turned to face him. "Did he hurt you?" he said.

Bobbi's words caught in her throat and she looked away from Lance. She thanked Nikki for checking in and told her to have fun with Todd. Then she whispered into the phone that she would get her back for sending Lance. And Lance heard every word she said.

"Did he hurt you?" Lance repeated.

Bobbi handed Lance back his phone, debating on how to answer his question.

"Look." She sighed. "I appreciate you coming to check on me and everything, but this has nothing to do with you." Bobbi touched Lance's arm in an attempt to show her gratitude but also to let him know to back off.

"Do you know how worried Nikki had to be to call me—a man she's only met a handful of times? Be grateful that you have a friend like her . . . and a friend like me, who cares enough to make sure you're okay when you don't answer your phone."

Taken aback, Bobbi put her hands on her hips and bucked her eyes at Lance. "Excuse me? But I didn't ask you to come over. And as you can see . . . I'm fine. So you can leave now."

Lance stared down at Bobbi and shook his head. "Stop being sassy."

Bobbi chuckled. "No one uses that word anymore." His humor relaxed her. "Thank you for being concerned, but I'm a big girl—I can take care of myself. Now, go back to work." Bobbi pushed Lance down the hallway and out the door.

<hr />

Bobbi pulled her sweater together and walked the three blocks to Ruth's office. Her appointment had been scheduled for noon, but thanks to a chronic lack of parking in the District, she happened to be running late.

When Bobbi arrived at the building, she checked her watch and went inside. She couldn't help that she was ten minutes late, and hoped that Ruth wouldn't need to reschedule.

Ruth greeted Bobbi with a hug. "How are you, my dear?"

"I'm well. Sorry I'm late." Bobbi's palms and feet started to sweat thinking about the things she wanted to share with Ruth. How could she tell this church-going sister that she'd just had an abortion? The last thing she needed was judgment.

"No worries," said Ruth. "We have an hour before my next appointment." Ruth sat down in a chair across from Bobbi. "So what's weighing heavy on your heart today?"

With one eye open and the other closed, Bobbi said, "Savon and I got back together." She held her breath waiting for Ruth's reaction. When she didn't get one, she exhaled and continued. "Things were going well until I found out I was pregnant a few weeks ago. But Savon said he didn't want kids—not even the child I was carrying. So . . . I had an abortion." Just then Bobbi got a flashback of herself, inserting the pills. She reached for tissues in the box on Ruth's desk.

The tears started and Bobbi dropped her head. Ruth went to Bobbi and held her until she stopped crying. When Ruth returned to her seat, her own heart ached for the torn young woman. There had been so much hurt in her life this year. Bobbi had been through a lot. Her heart had been through a lot.

"So, I take it the abortion wasn't your choice?" said Ruth.

"No. But I didn't know what else to do after Savon said he didn't want kids. When I started thinking about having a baby on my own, I panicked. I couldn't see myself doing it alone. Then I thought about what people would say about me—especially not being married." Bobbi shook her head. "I just couldn't see it."

Ruth said a silent prayer for Bobbi, Savon and the child before responding. "I'm so sorry for your loss. That had to be a very hard and hurtful decision to make." Ruth's head tilted to the side. "Are you and Savon still together?"

"Heck, no. He doesn't deserve me. His attitude was almost smug when I tried to reason with him about the whole thing—it felt like he gave me an ultimatum." Bobbi looked away. "I can't believe what I did . . . to my baby." Her words trailed off. "I hate Savon."

"You know Bobbi, in this situation, no one wins—not even Savon. Remember when we met earlier in the year and I told you it was important to tell yourself the truth? Well, let's practice that now." Ruth scooted to the edge of her seat. "The truth is, you are a loving person who made a difficult decision out of hurt and also out of fear and shame. But that does not make you a bad person."

Bobbi wiped at warm tears as she listened to Ruth, soaking in her words. This is why she'd come. She needed this comfort.

"The best thing you can do for yourself," said Ruth, "is learn from this experience so you won't find yourself addressing the same issue again in the future." Ruth's gaze became more intense. "Have you asked God to forgive you?"

"Yes. But I don't know if that's possible. I know I did the unthinkable . . ."

"Beloved, God says that when we ask for forgiveness, he forgives us. So believe it. Don't beat up on yourself or allow guilt to overtake you." Ruth went to sit next to Bobbi and rested a hand on top of hers. "Have you forgiven Savon?"

Bobbi's neck jerked back. Ruth was asking for a parting-of-the-red-sea miracle. "How can I?" she said. "He's the reason I need therapy in the first place."

"My dear. Here's another truth moment. It took both of you to get to this point. Own your part of the breakdown in the relationship. You can't change him, but you can change you." Ruth looked at her watch and patted Bobbi's hand. "Our time is up." She smiled. "Let's meet again next week to talk about healthy relationships. Okay?"

"Okay." Bobbi smiled back—grateful for Ruth.

"Let's pray before you leave," said Ruth, and she bowed her head. "Father God in heaven, thank you for this beautiful woman of God. I lift her up before you, God—her Maker and Creator. Heal her heart, God. Heal the memories and emotions of her past. Create within her a new heart—one that knows love and feels loved and believes in love. Lord, I thank you for forgiveness. Thank you for your compassion toward her, and your mercies that are new every morning. I speak peace to her thoughts, to her mind, and to her heart. In Jesus's name I pray. Amen!"

That night, Ruth sat in her favorite purple chair with a cup of coffee, reflecting over her meeting with Bobbi. Seeing the sadness in the young woman's eyes and hearing the pain in her cry had tugged greatly at Ruth's heart. Bobbi was such a smart lady, and quite shrewd in business, but her heart hadn't been trained in the ways of love.

There were rules to love. Love requires sacrifice and commitment. Love does not behave in a way that is careless. Love is strong—it endures the tests and trials of life. Love can handle change and the unexpected things that life brings—it will always adjust. Love hangs in there for the long haul. Love thinks about the other person—it serves the other person.

Ruth sipped her coffee. So many of the young women she counseled had never experienced that kind of love. Not in childhood or as an adult.

Getting to know Bobbi reminded Ruth of herself twenty years ago. It had taken years for her to forgive her self for the same bad decisions—to understand love, and to believe that God had forgiven her and loved her no less. Ruth wiped at a lone tear and logged into her email account to send Bobbi a note.

Dearest Bobbi,

I hope this note finds you feeling much better. Thank you for sharing your heart with me today. It's not so easy to talk about hurtful things when you're vulnerable. You are a courageous and resilient woman, and I admire the fighter in you.

I want you to understand this about love: Sometimes it will hurt—not because someone didn't care about you, rather, people love you the best way they know how. At some point and time, we have all been hurt by someone's love for us—parents, friends, family—we have all been casualties of love. Even with the best intentions, sometimes we just hurt each other.

But that's where forgiveness comes in. I mentioned forgiving Savon in our session and I really want you to work toward that. Trust me when I say, before he leaves this earth, if he has a conscience at all, he will have to face his indiscretions. So, don't let those hurt feelings turn into hate or bitterness. You're far too fabulous for that. ☺

Moving forward, if you need to, grieve the loss of your unborn child. Allow your self to let go of the pain and purge the grief. Please, please, please forgive yourself and believe that God has forgiven you and loves you the same.

Be blessed my love, and take care.
Sister Ruth

After sending the email, Ruth climbed in bed with her husband and asked him to hold her tight. She needed comforting tonight. All the women she counseled were hurting and broken. They wanted love and were trying everything to increase their chances. Ruth shed tears for Bobbi and for all the other hurting women she counseled, until she fell asleep in her husband's arms.

Chapter 24

Bobbi printed the email from Ruth and powered down her laptop. The counselor's concern for her meant so much. Right now, she didn't have the support of the two women closest to her because she still couldn't bring herself to tell them how reckless she'd been. So Ruth's words meant everything to her—they helped her stay sane.

She read Ruth's note over and over again. Forgiving Savon would be hard. Even though she didn't want anything more to do with him, she'd expected to hear from him by now.

Bobbi's phone rang and her stomach twisted in knots. She reached over to get it and looked at the caller-id. It was Lance. Bobbi frowned and rejected the call. He'd already called twice and left a message. She'd listen later and get back to him.

Back in the office the following week, Bobbi called a meeting with Ciara to go over her schedule. She'd been working from home for almost two weeks, and it was time to move forward.

After the meeting, Bobbi called Lance. He'd left a voice message a few days ago inviting her to his daughter's birthday party. Bobbi hadn't called him back until now because she didn't want to answer any questions about the day he'd showed up at her house, thanks to Nikki.

Bobbi left a message for Lance and pressed on with her day. She had a meeting with Sweet Feet later that afternoon to discuss rumors about him cheating on his fiancée and her trying to run him over with a car. It had been the top story at an Atlanta based celebrity gossip website. Bobbi loved her clients, but she wished they would keep their turkey sausages in their pants.

When Lance called back, he asked Bobbi to come by his office when she had time—he had something he wanted to show her.

At ten after five, Bobbi headed up to Lance's office. Inside Holder Enterprises, she stood in the waiting area, admiring the framed, life-sized newspaper articles chronicling Lance's business success.

"Hey, Bobbi," he said, walking up behind her.

She turned around. "Hey, what's up?"

They had a quick embrace and Lance said, "Follow me. I wanna show you something."

In his office, Lance pulled up pictures of Ava on his desktop and motioned for Bobbi to come and see. Saturday would be Ava's fourth birthday and he wanted Bobbi to be there.

"Awww . . . she's a doll baby," said Bobbi. "And she looks like you." *Hmmm.*

"Thank you," said the proud dad. "Can you make the party?"

Bobbi smiled. "Uh . . . sure. Just text me the time and address."

"Uhm . . . you should also know that it's a family barbecue," he added, waiting for her reaction.

Great. "Okay." Bobbi hunched her shoulders. "I'll be there." She forced a wider smile and went to sit in the chair across from his desk.

The two talked for a while longer, catching up on life, and Lance even mentioned that he'd been spending time with Lil Dizzy. If Bobbi questioned it before, she didn't any longer. This man liked her—and not like a sister.

Nonetheless, Bobbi needed to get back to her office and shut things down for the day. Lance walked her out with his arm draped over her shoulder. This was new. Bobbi looked up at him and the two chuckled at the gesture.

At the elevator bank, Bobbi pressed the button and then faced Lance. "What should I get Ava for her birthday." When Bobbi was Ava's age, she loved baby dolls. But she didn't know if that were the case for a twenty-first century four-year-old.

When Lance moved his arm from around Bobbi's shoulder, she glanced over at the group of men talking in front of the sports agency. To her surprise, Savon and John the freelance agent she'd introduced him to, along with the owner of Hollister Sports Agency, were standing less than ten yards away. John and the agency owner nodded their heads toward her and she forced a smile, but Savon just stared—and so did Bobbi for a moment, then she looked away.

Lance observed their silent exchange, and his body tensed up until he saw the sadness in Bobbi's eyes. Then he stared Savon down—his fingers curling into a fist. Bobbi grabbed Lance by the hand and pulled, letting the elevator open and close, but he wouldn't budge.

"Uh, I left something in your office," Bobbi said, tugging at his arm.

Lance pulled his eyes off of Savon to look at Bobbi, and then followed her lead. Bobbi pushed him ahead of her into his suite and then looked over her shoulder. She couldn't believe that Savon had gone back to talking with the other men like nothing had happened. How could she have ever believed he cared about her?

"So, what did you leave?" said Lance, frowning. He already knew she hadn't left anything because she didn't come with anything.

"What?" said Bobbi, pretending to be confused.

"Was that flower boy?"

"Uhm . . . yeah." Bobbi swallowed a laugh.

"Is he the reason you called Nikki in Jamaica and she sent me to check on you?"

"I don't want to get into that right now, but yes. We broke up and I needed to talk to someone, so I called Nikki. That's what girlfriends do."

Lance looked into Bobbi's eyes and then went to sit behind his desk.

Bobbi felt bad. She'd caused Lance enough trouble for one day. "I'm leaving now," she said. "But send me a picture of Ava. And oh . . . what should I get for her birthday?"

"Anything," said Lance, getting up from his desk. "I'm going with you to your office."

"You don't have to, but if you must—come on." Bobbi hoped Savon and his crew were gone. But no matter what, she would be going back to her office.

Lance followed Bobbi out and they rode the elevator to her floor. "You want me to follow you home?" he said. Lance had been glad to see that her ex had gone, but that didn't mean Bobbi would be safe.

"No, Lance," said Bobbi when the elevator opened on her floor. "You need to go home too. I'll be fine." Bobbi didn't let him get off. She gave him a hug and sent him on his way.

When Bobbi made it to her office suite and stuck the key in the lock, she felt someone walk up behind her.

"Hey."

Bobbi spun around at the sound of his voice but she didn't say anything.

"You're not gonna speak to me?" Savon said with a smirk on his face, his hands stuffed in his pockets.

"What do you want," she said, holding the chrome door handle.

"You really don't want to talk to me?" said Savon.

"No, I don't."

Savon looked away, breaking the awkward gaze between them. "Uhm . . . it's good seeing you. You look good." He reached his hand to brush against her face, but she leaned the other way.

"I have to go," she said. "Goodbye." She pulled the heavy glass door open and locked it behind her, leaving Savon standing on the other side.

"Bye," said Savon under his breath, wondering how long Bobbi would be in her feelings about this whole thing.

An hour later, Bobbi packed up and left work. On the drive home, she still didn't understand why Savon had been in her building with John. When she had introduced the two, John was a freelance agent and he didn't work in her building. So none of this made sense. But most of all, how dare Savon, think he could roll up on her by accident and get some conversation, after giving her the silent treatment for weeks.

Pulling into the garage, Bobbi counted herself lucky to have Lance as a friend. He'd been her protector in his own way, and boy did it feel good. She defended other people for a living. But it was rare to experience someone standing up for her.

After dinner, Bobbi called Nikki to tell her about her man drama. "Girl, you will never believe what happened today." Bobbi smacked her lips. "I thought Savon and Lance were gonna go to blows in my building."

"Say whaaat?! What happened?"

"I guess Savon had a meeting at the sports agency and by co-inky-dink, I was leaving Lance's office when Savon and his agent and another guy where standing in the hallway talking."

"Then what happened? You're talking too slow. Go!" said Nikki.

"You know I haven't talked to Savon in at least three weeks, right? Well, when we saw each other, we just stared—and I guess Lance didn't like it because he looked like a lion about to attack." Bobbi grinned. "I had to get Lance outta there."

"Why was he so upset? Did Savon say something?"

"Wait a minute. I just got a text from Savon," said Bobbi."

"What does he want?" said Nikki.

"He wants to know if we can talk." Bobbi closed her texting app. "I wish I would."

"I'm glad to see you sticking to your guns this time. That ninja must've messed up real bad." Nikki chuckled.

The best friends talked a while longer and then Bobbi went to bed. Around midnight, her phone rang.

"Yes, Savon?"

"Who was dude with you today?"

"Why?"

"Cause I wanna know."

"I haven't heard from you in weeks and you think you have the right to ask me about someone else? If that's what you called for, goodbye."

"Wait . . . that's not the only reason I called." Savon paused. "So what are you going to do about the situation—the baby?" It made him nervous to bring up the topic, but his life depended on it.

"You don't have to worry," she said. "I've taken care of that."

"You got the abortion?" he said, his voice an octave higher.

"Yes."

Savon breathed a sigh of relief. "Uhm . . . I'm sorry you had to do that without me. Maybe we can sit down and talk things through. I miss you."

Shaking her head, surprised yet again by the magnitude of his selfishness, Bobbi said, "Please don't call me anymore. I hate what you did and I really do hate you right now." Bobbi ended the call, wondering if he was on crack.

Chapter 25

Bobbi said a prayer and then knocked on Lance's front door. When it swung open, what Bobbi had assumed was now confirmed.

"Hi. Can I help you?" said the young woman who answered the door.

"Hi. I'm Bobbi. Is Lance here?"

Just then Lance walked up. "Heyyy, Bobbi. Come on in."

"This is my niece Mackenzie," he said, closing the door. "I'm glad you could make it." Ava ran up to Lance and grabbed his leg. "And this is Ava—the birthday girl."

"It's nice to meet you both Mackenzie and Ava." Bobbi handed the little girl a gift bag. "Happy birthday."

"Thank you," said Ava, taking the bag with one hand and still holding her father's leg with the other.

"Hey, don't I know you?" Mackenzie said. "You look familiar."

Lance frowned, looking between Bobbi and Mackenzie. "You know each other?"

Bobbi spoke up. "I think I can clear this up. Earlier this year, I was at a restaurant, and Ava came running into the restroom when I opened the door to leave out."

"Oh, yeaahh," said Mackenzie. "That was you." She turned to Ava. "Do you remember her, Ava?"

Ava looked at Bobbi. "Yes," she said. "You stopped me from falling, right?"

Bobbi chuckled. "That's right."

"Well, I guess I didn't need to introduce you to them," said Lance, in disbelief. "Come on so you can meet everybody else—unless you already know them too."

Bobbi laughed and followed Lance to the family room where she met his family and friends, and Mackenzie took Ava back to the birthday party in the basement.

Lance stayed by Bobbi's side for the first hour after her arrival. But when the birthday party wound down and the kids began to leave, Lance went to see their guests out. Meanwhile, Ava made her way to the family room and went to sit near Bobbi holding the doll she'd given her.

"Miss Bobbi, thank you for the doll. Do you want to see all my presents?"

"You're welcome, Ava. I would love to see your presents."

Ava grabbed Bobbi's hand and led her to the basement. When they got to the bottom of the stairs, Bobbi had another surprise.

"What's up, Miss B?" said Lil Dizzy, taking a break from the video game.

"Hey, Dizzy! What are you doing here?" She embraced him.

"Mister L, invited me to the party."

"That's nice." Bobbi smiled at the young man and rubbed his back.

"I'm going to get a burger," he said, and headed upstairs.

Thirty minutes later, Lance came to the basement looking for Bobbi and found Ava sitting on Bobbi's lap brushing her dolls hair.

"I've been looking for you," said Lance. He winked at Bobbi. "I thought you had snuck out on me."

Bobbi smiled. "I've seen all of Ava's toys and now we're watching Frozen." She smiled at Ava.

"Yeah, dad. We watching Frozen."

"Okay, little one. I need to talk to Miss Bobbi. Go upstairs with grandma."

"I don't want to," said Ava, pouting.

Lance pointed. "Go."

Ava jumped off of Bobbi's lap and cried as she mounted the stairs.

Lance sat down next to Bobbi on the sofa and put his arm around her shoulder. Bobbi didn't know how to respond to him in the moment so she forced a smile. Her thoughts were all over the place. Seeing Lance in his element turned her on. He had a wonderful family, a sweet daughter, and he made her feel at home.

"So," said Bobbi, "what did you do with the old Dizzy? He's a different kid."

Lance looked into her eyes and said, "Love and respect . . . that's it."

At eight o'clock, Bobbi told Lance that she had to leave. She'd been there for hours and didn't want to outstay her welcome. She went to tell everyone goodbye, especially Ava, and she told Dizzy that she would see him later.

Lance walked Bobbi to her car and she gave him an envelope. It was a gift certificate to a spa for three deep tissue massage sessions. When Lance opened it, he looked puzzled, and Bobbi burst out laughing.

"I saw how tight you got when we were standing at the elevator by your office earlier this week, and figured you could use a massage. You need to relax, man." She chuckled.

"So you got jokes, huh?" Lance laughed and pulled Bobbi into an embrace. He kissed the top of her head and exhaled a deep breath.

Bobbi cleared her throat and looked up at Lance. "Guess I should be going."

Lance opened her door. "Can we do lunch after church tomorrow?"

"Sure."

"Drive safe, and let me know when you make it home," Lance said before closing the door.

The next morning, Lance stood outside the church talking with a friend. When he saw Bobbi walking towards him in a crowd, he reached for her arm.

"Wait for me," he said.

Bobbi smiled and nodded toward Lance and told Nikki she'd meet her inside.

Lance ended his conversation and went to give Bobbi a more proper greeting. He hugged her and kissed her cheek. "We still on for lunch?"

"Yes." Bobbi pulled her coat together. "Let's go inside—it's chilly." She looped her arm through Lance's and they went inside to find Nikki.

After service, Bobbi insisted they take separate cars and meet up at the restaurant. She needed her own wheels in case Lance got weird, especially since she didn't know what he wanted to talk about.

At lunch, Lance got straight to the point once they were seated. He reached for Bobbi's hand.

"I want to be with you," he said. "I want you to be my lady. I want to see if you and I can work in a relationship."

Bobbi's free hand covered her mouth and her eyes blinked slow and hard as she searched for the right words. "Uhh . . . I don't know what to say. I didn't expect this."

"Are you saying you didn't know I like you?"

"No, I'm not saying that. I finally picked up on that. It's the part about wanting a relationship that has me in shock."

Lance took both of Bobbi's hands in his and shared his feelings with her. He told Bobbi that he knew who she was the day he changed her flat tire, thanks to a picture that Grace had shown him before he moved to DC. But he didn't say anything because she hadn't reached out to him like her mother had said she would, and he didn't want to be a bother. However, when they started spending time together, he knew she was the one for him. And the lasting impression she'd made on Ava had been an unexpected bonus.

"So, Bobbi," said Lance, gently rubbing his thumbs over her fingers. "What I'm saying is, I want you to get to know the man I am. And I look forward to learning more about the woman you are. What do you say?"

Bobbi's heart pounded and she bit down on her lip. "You sure do know how to surprise a girl. Wow. Uhm . . . I'm flattered. And I really do appreciate you. But I have to be honest. I don't know if I'm ready for another relationship so fast. I mean—I just got out of one that really took everything out of me."

"So, are you saying, no?" he said.

"No," Bobbi blurted, caressing the hands that held hers. "What I'm saying is, let me take some time to think about it. Okay?"

Lance looked deep into Bobbi's eyes. "Okay. But can we continue to get to know each other until you decide if you're ready for more?" he said.

"Of course. You can't get rid of me that easy."

Bobbi and Lance finished lunch and then crossed the street to go to the shopping center. Lance had grabbed Bobbi by the hand when they stepped off the curb and still hadn't let go. Bobbi let him do his thing and she followed. Hand-in-hand they strolled through the mall window-shopping until Lance led her into the Gucci store.

"Which one do you like?" he said, as they browsed the handbags.

"I like this one," Bobbi said, admiring the bag she had on her must-have list for Christmas.

Lance motioned for the sales lady and asked her to giftwrap the purse.

"Who's that for," said Bobbi.

"For you," he said, squeezing her hand. "It's for your birthday."

"My birthday? How'd you know my birthday is this week?" Bobbi felt her knees knock together.

"Don't worry about that."

When the sales clerk handed the wrapped box over the counter, Lance took it and gave it to Bobbi. "Happy, early birthday."

Bobbi thanked the sales clerk and then turned to Lance. "You are so thoughtful. Thank you for my bag." She reached for Lance's face and pecked his lips, knowing that her gesture, on some level, meant she'd accepted his offer for them to be more than friends. And she was okay with that because he'd been turning her on and blowing her mind, one moment at a time.

Bobbi called Nikki on her way home and screamed when she picked up.

"What the heck? Stop screaming in my ear."

"Girl, you'll never guess what. He wants to be with me and said he knew I was the one all along, and that he wants me to know what kind of man he is, and—" Bobbi was talking so fast she swallowed wrong and couldn't stop coughing.

"What are you doing," said Nikki, while Bobbi tried to clear her throat. "Why are you talking so fast, and who the heck are you talking about?"

Bobbi managed to get out a laugh. "Okay," she said with choppy breaths. "At lunch, Lance basically told me that he's been feeling me since we met, and he wants us to be in a relationship!" Bobbi screamed again.

"That's wonderful, B. I'm so happy for you! But why in the heck do you keep screaming like that?" said Nikki.

"Because I didn't know until today that I want all of it. I want marriage and babies and Lance and Ava. I want love . . . real love. And I believe Lance is the one to give it to me."

"Did you tell him that?"

"Not yet, but I will. Oh, and girrrll." She smacked her lips and her body broke into dance from the waist up as she drove. "He bought me that Gucci bag I had my eyes on. Said it was for my birthday."

"What?! No way!"

"Yes, way. The one we were both looking at."

"Now that's what I'm talking bout. Lance knows what to do for a woman. You'd better not let him get away."

When Bobbi arrived at home, she took off her church clothes and called her mom. Grace would scream as loud as Bobbi had when she heard the news.

"Ma, today Lance told me that he wants us to be in a relationship. Can you believe it?"

"Awww . . . I'm so happy for you, honey. I'm glad he finally told you," said Grace.

"What do you mean," said Bobbi, frowning.

Grace grinned. "He told me weeks ago that he really liked you but he didn't know what to do because you were in a relationship. So, I told him to be patient and everything would work out. And judging from the excitement in your voice, sounds like it did."

Bobbi's mouth hung open. "I can't believe you didn't tell me this. Why didn't you tell me?"

"Because it wasn't my place. And besides, he already did. Be happy, girl." Grace chuckled.

Bobbi shook her head and laughed too. "Bye, Ma. I'll call you later."

Before they hung up, Grace told Bobbi that Lance was a good man and that she needed to give it a chance to really get to know him and his daughter. She encouraged Bobbi to leave the past in its proper place and to move forward being hopeful and excited about the future—being careful not to make Lance pay for the misbehavior of other men. Grace told her daughter to give Lance and herself a chance.

Bobbi washed a bowl of grapes and went to the family room. Two of the most important people in her life had confirmed that she should consider being with Lance. But she also wondered what Ruth would say since the counselor knew things about her recent life the other two didn't. Nonetheless, she wouldn't bother Ruth tonight. She'd make that call tomorrow.

So Bobbi snuggled up on the sofa watching TV and surfing the web. When she logged into her email account, she had another surprise. The email from Ruth read:

Dear Bobbi,

Although we weren't able to connect last week for our talk about healthy relationships, I wanted to share a few things for you to consider.

No one can meet all of our expectations—it is impossible—and it is an unfair burden to place on another human being. Yet there remains something to be said for having standards. For example, if you want a man to be supportive of your faith, your career, and your interests, then you must look for those qualities in the men you date. If you want a responsible man, then observe how a man handles his own affairs. If family and respect are important to you, then pay attention to the way a man relates to his mother (especially) and to his own relatives. Decide what really means something to you and set your standards.

Beloved, I know you're not content with having relationships that are void of commitment. So, stir up your faith in love. Hope again . . . believe in love again. Tell yourself the truth about what you want from a man . . . and try love again.

No more lies. No more allowing lies to steal your joy, and kill your hopes and dreams. If love makes you a casualty—if it hurts you—then so be it, because then you'll have an opportunity to demonstrate forgiveness and patience and kindness, which will mature you in your faith and strengthen your heart. Remember, love never fails.

When you're ready, let's arrange a time to discuss these things further.

I love you,
Ruth

Speechless, Bobbi smiled as a warm tear trickled down her face. What perfect timing for Ruth's note. Now she had to call Ruth. There was no way she could get to sleep tonight without telling Ruth her news and hearing the counselor's advice. Ruth answered on the second ring.

"Hi, Sister Ruth. Hope I'm not disturbing you."

"Hi, Bobbi. You're not disturbing me. Gerald and I were just having a cup of coffee. What's going on, dear?"

"Well, today after church, Lance—do you know Lance Holder? He's a member at New Covenant." Bobbi continued as if Ruth had said she knew him. "He asked me to be in a relationship with him, and I do like him, but I wanted to know if you think it's too soon to get emotionally involved after my breakup with Savon—and of course the other thing?"

Ruth smiled, although Bobbi couldn't see it. "My dear, what do you think? Do you think it's too soon? Because no matter what Lance wants, you must want him too. Otherwise, the relationship is a disaster waiting to happen down the road. But, personally speaking, I believe your heart is ready for love. It's been a long, hard year for you and you've worked through the pain. So if you like this man and the way he treats you, and you enjoy his company, and you feel safe with him, I'd say that your heart could use some love."

And there it was—the third confirmation. Bobbi didn't realize she'd been holding her breath until Ruth finished speaking. "I think, I want to give it a chance," said Bobbi. Excitement and peace washed over her. "Because of Lance, now I know what I want—and that is love and a family."

Bobbi chatted briefly with Ruth about the email and the irony of the timing and thanked her for always saying what she needed to hear. Then Ruth prayed with Bobbi.

"Oh, before we hang up," said Ruth, "yes, I know Lance. He's a wonderful young man and so is his daughter. My husband and I know them personally." Ruth reflected on the mysterious ways of God before adding, "Okay, love. I'll talk to you later. Good night."

Chapter 26

Two months later, Bobbi lay in Lance's arms while Ava opened her Christmas presents. They were waiting for Ava to finish opening hers before passing gifts to each other.

Bobbi whispered, "I love you," to Lance and he kissed her.

"Stop telling me that, woman." Lance rubbed her thigh under the blanket when Ava wasn't looking. He found it impossible to keep his hands off of her, and it didn't help that she had been showing him how much she cared about him. But Lance had promised his church mentor, Gerald that he would wait until marriage to sleep with Bobbi.

Bobbi had agreed to do the same, so they were on one accord. This would be the first time either of them had practiced abstinence in a relationship, but they both wanted something to look forward to if they got married.

When Lance gave Bobbi her present, she stared at the small red box and her armpits became wet. She looked at Lance and then at Ava, who started jumping up and down, telling her to open it. Bobbi removed the white bow and opened the box to reveal a sparkly five-carat diamond set in platinum. Tears fell before she had a chance to say anything. She watched Lance take the ring out of the box and bend down on one knee.

"Bobbi. Will you marry me?"

Ava repeated after her father. "Yeah, Miss Bobbi, will you marry us . . . will you marry us?"

"Yes, Lance." Bobbi held his face. "I will marry you." She puckered her lips, touched by his tenderness, and kissed him.

"And yes, Ava, I will marry you too." Bobbi pulled the little girl into her arms and squeezed her tight.

"Group hug," said Bobbi as she reached for Lance.

Ava struggled to put her arms around both of them, grunting and reaching wide until Lance and Bobbi pulled her into their embrace, laughing and planting kisses all over her sweet little face.

The doorbell rang and Mackenzie went to answer it with Ava in tow. She let Lil Dizzy in and he scooped up Ava in his arms and then followed Mackenzie back to the family room.

"Merry Christmas," said Bobbi when Dizzy entered the room. She hugged him.

"Merry Christmas," Miss B, said Dizzy.

"Merry Christmas, man" said Lance when Bobbi stepped aside.

"Merry Christmas, Mister L."

Dizzy and Lance did the man embrace and handshake thing while Bobbi admired the love and respect—her eyes brimming with tears.

"Look at what I got for Christmas," said Bobbi, wiggling her fingers toward Dizzy.

Dizzy congratulated Lance with a fist-pound and then hugged Bobbi again. Then Lance rubbed Dizzy's head and asked him to freestyle eight bars for love—a man's love for his woman. He'd been mentoring and coaching Lil Dizzy in these areas.

"Okay, Mister L, here it goes. Uh . . . uh . . .

"You still the sexiest I ever been around: beautiful hair, skin light brown,
smile that could light up a room, beautiful like flowers in the spring you bloom.
Ask me for anything—say it, it's yours: Gucci, Louis, Michael Kors.
You look the same today as you did when I met you—
you're special, nothin' short of incredible.
Happy I met you, could never forget you,
I got you for life, put that on mine.
I got you covered 'til the end of time!"

"My boy!" said Lance, slapping him on the back. "That's what I'm talkin' bout. This boy got skills."

Bobbi blushed. "Thank you, Dizzy." She kissed the young man on the cheek. It warmed her heart to see the tremendous change in Dizzy's life in such a short time.

Then Bobbi kissed her man and gave him a look that made his whole body tingle. In that moment, they both knew the engagement couldn't be long. Shucks, if it were up to Lance, the ceremony would be today. Who needed to be engaged for a year?

Bobbi didn't know how she could prepare for a wedding in a week. Her and Nikki's dresses would be off the rack, given the short notice, and she had to get her mom and step-dad here to give her away. Things were happening so fast, but Bobbi couldn't be happier. After Christmas dinner, Lance had asked if she would be okay with them starting their marriage journey sooner, rather than later. He wanted them to exchange wedding vows on New Year's Day!

At first, she'd thought he meant the following year, as in three hundred and sixty-five days away. But when he said, next weekend—it took all she could do not to faint right there at the dinner table.

Right now, Bobbi sat outside Nikki's condo going over her to-do list while she waited for Nikki to come down. The wedding was in five days and both their dresses needed minor alterations, which the seamstress said she could get done by Saturday, the day before the wedding.

Nikki got in the car, and the first thing she did was reach for Bobbi's hand.

"Girrrll, that ring is everything." Nikki moved Bobbi's finger from side to side admiring the brilliance and clarity of the stone. "He must really love you. Humph. Be ready to give it up when, how, and anywhere he wants it to earn that rock."

Bobbi laughed. "I'm ready now! Trust and believe that."

"Right?" Nikki chuckled. She still couldn't believe Bobbi would be married in a few days!

Bobbi's phone rang as she pulled into traffic and her car's Bluetooth connected the call. When the name Nutcracker showed on the display screen in her instrument panel, Nikki looked at Bobbi and burst out laughing. Bobbi chuckled and told her it was Savon. She'd been ignoring his calls for weeks because she'd already told him they were done countless times. But now she needed to get rid of him. Bobbi put the call on speaker.

"Hello."

"Uhm . . . hey, Bobbi. Can we talk?"

"About what, Savon?

"About us," he said. "About business. I miss you. You won't answer my calls or texts. Why are you still mad? What happened is over, so we should be able to move on. And I—"

"Let me stop you right there, homeboy. You and me—we will never be good. I gave you everything—you got the best of me. And when things got tough, you bailed out. I would never have done that to you. I stuck by you and believed in you when nobody else did. Humph. But the best thing you could ever have done for me is to turn your back on me. It showed me all I needed to see. I see you."

"Where is all of this coming from?" said Savon. "I had hoped we would be good by now. John and I are making some big moves with my career and I want you to be part of it. That's why you saw me at Hollister a couple of months ago."

"What?!" Bobbi grunted. "I can't with you . . . I just can't." She ended the call.

Nikki frowned, looking at Bobbi. "Are you okay?" Now Nikki knew for sure that whatever had happened between Bobbi and Savon while she was in Jamaica had been pretty serious. "You wanna talk about it?"

Bobbi pulled into a parking space at the bridal shop and turned off the car. "No, I'm good," she said, massaging her temples. "I just can't deal with that fool. He's so selfish." She took a minute to calm her nerves and then apologized to Nikki for all the drama.

Inside the shop, Bobbi convinced Nikki to do her fitting first. So the seamstress took Nikki to the dressing room, and Bobbi walked off in the opposite direction and called Savon back.

"Savon, listen to me. I do not want to hear from you again. What we had is over. I don't want to get back with you personally or professionally. Am I clear?"

"But why? People have problems in their relationships all the time, and they work it out."

"We will never work out what happened between us—you bring out the worst in me. And just so you know, I'm engaged now, so it would be disrespectful for you to call or text me again. Goodbye."

Chapter 27

Saturday morning, Lance picked up Bobbi and they went for a couples massage. Family and friends were still arriving in town and they wanted to spend some time alone before things got even more hectic.

"I can't believe we'll be married tomorrow," said Lance, his taut muscles surrendering to the pressure of the deep tissue massage.

Bobbi's body tensed at his words and the masseuse asked if she was okay. She nodded and the woman continued to knead the knots in her shoulders.

"It's pretty surreal," agreed Bobbi. "But, uhhh . . . are you sure about all of this?" She sat up and asked both massage therapists to give them a moment. When they left, she continued. "This is so sudden, I'm just concerned that we're not ready for something so permanent." The anxiety and reality of everything had Bobbi OD'ing on sweets and second-guessing everything.

Lance popped up off the table. "What do you mean? You don't want to marry me?" he said with frown lines forming on his brow.

Bobbi went to him. "No. I'm not saying that. It's just that I question whether I'm ready and if we know each other well enough." She rubbed his arms. "You don't think about that?"

"No, I don't. I've been waiting for this moment since I met you face-to-face. I didn't think I had a chance after I found out you were in a relationship, but I had people in my corner who told me to hang in there." He stood up and lifted Bobbi's chin to look into her eyes. "I want to be with you. We can make it work, but you have to be willing, too. Do you want to be with me?"

Bobbi blinked and a tear fell. "Yes. I want to be with you."

Later that night at the rehearsal dinner, the bride and groom to-be and their wedding party sat at the head table listening as Lance's best man made a toast. When Nikki stood up and waited for her turn to do the same, she saw Savon peeking through the back door of the fellowship hall. So she whispered to Todd and they excused themselves from the table and went to deal with Savon.

"What are you doing here?" said Nikki. "Bobbi told you to leave her alone."

"Bobbi and I were just in a relationship," said Savon, his eyes glassy and red. "I came to see for myself if what I've heard is true." His voice cracked. "Can you tell her to come out here?"

"Are you crazy?" said Nikki. She looked at Todd and then added, "You need to leave. Now."

"You heard her," said Todd. "It's time to go, bruh."

Seconds later, the door swung open and Lance stormed into the hallway. "What's going on?" he said, looking between Nikki and Todd and Savon. "Why are you here, man?" Lance gritted through clenched teeth, standing within inches of Savon's face.

Lance looked over at Nikki and motioned for them to leave. So Nikki grabbed Todd's hand and hurried back into the fellowship hall.

Nikki made it back to the table just in time. Bobbi had left her seat to go find Lance. So Nikki wrapped her arm around Bobbi's waist and guided her back to her chair and they sat down.

"You don't want to go out there," said Nikki. "Your man is giving Savon some act-right. Just chill. He'll be back." A nervous grin escaped Nikki's mouth as she patted Bobbi's leg.

"What do you mean? Savon is here?" Bobbi gave Nikki a wild-eyed look and threw up her hands. "What the heck is going on? Where is Lance?" Bobbi wanted to scream but she didn't want to draw any more attention to the craziness that had started when Nikki and Todd had left the table so abruptly, followed by Lance barreling from the table like the Incredible Hulk. Everyone had been watching her to see what she would do. That's when Lance's father—God bless his soul—stood up and started telling funny stories about Lance's childhood to distract from the three-ring circus. Bobbi looked at Nikki with a straight face. "I'm going to find Lance."

"No, Bobbi. Just wait," said Nikki.

Just then Lance came back into the room and took his seat. All eyes in the room were on him. Whispers could be heard across the fellowship hall. Nikki looked down the table at Lance, wondering what he'd done with Savon, and Bobbi didn't know what to think.

"Don't you have something to tell me?" said Bobbi.

Lance turned to face her. "Flower boy thought he was coming to see you and talk to you—my wife—on our night. Get outta here with that!" Lance threw up his hand. "But I got him straight though," he said, nodding his head.

Concern now etched in Bobbi's face, she wanted to know more. "Is that it? I wanna know what happened?"

Bobbi watched Lance gulp down his champagne and then lean to the other side and whisper to his best man who then got up and left the table.

"Bae," he said. "It's handled, so don't worry about it. Tonight is about you and me and our family—our future." He breathed a deep sigh. "Trust me." Lance pulled Bobbi to him and kissed his wife to-be, and the room erupted in cheers.

The next morning, Grace and Nikki's mother chatted, and Ava played with her doll while Nikki helped Bobbi get into her dress. After Nikki zipped her up, Bobbi stepped into her sparkly silver pumps and went to look in the full-length mirror. She smoothed her hands over the front of the winter white, floor length gown. Her make-up and hair had been done thirty minutes ago, and she wore her mother's diamond necklace. Everything was perfect.

The image of the woman looking back at her had confidence and hope. She felt good about forgetting the former things and not dwelling on the past. She'd decided to accept the new things springing up all around her. The past didn't compare to the new life unfolding right before her eyes.

"Somebody get me a tissue, please," she said.

Ava snatched a tissue from the box and ran over to Bobbi. "Here, Miss Bobbi." Ava twisted from side to side causing her dress to flare out while she watched Bobbi. "You look beautiful."

"Thank you, sunshine." Bobbi smiled and brushed a finger against Ava's cheek.

Moments later, a knock came on the door and Ciara went to answer it. Ruth came in and greeted all the ladies and Ava with a hug and then pulled Bobbi aside.

"Are you ready, young lady?" said Ruth, holding Bobbi's hands and smiling. "I'm so happy for you."

"Yes, I'm ready." Bobbi matched her smile. "Last night, things got crazy, but it showed me the kind of man I have. I know Lance will protect me and that he loves me. So I'm willing to put in the work to have everything else."

"Okay, my love. That's what I wanted to hear." Ruth kissed her cheek. "See you at the altar."

Lance stood before the church, tears staining his brown skin as he watched the most beautiful woman in his world come toward him. Bobbi walked down the aisle focused on her man and humming along to the song "With You I'm Born Again"—the perfect metaphor for their love.

Her stepfather gave her away and then Bobbi joined hands with Lance at the altar. Bobbi looked to her left and smiled at Nikki and then down at little Ava, the flower girl—her heart full of joy. Even Lil Dizzy, with his big teenager self, had marched down the aisle carrying the ring.

Gerald and Ruth Abernathy officiated the wedding ceremony, and everyone Bobbi and Lance loved and who loved them were there to witness their vows. There wasn't a dry eye in the place after Lance professed his love for Bobbi. And once Bobbi shared her heart for her husband, sniffles could be heard throughout the sanctuary.

At the reception, during the mother-son dance, Bobbi sat at the sweetheart table alone, admiring her husband. No words could fully express the joy she felt today. Lance had pretty much orchestrated the entire wedding. He'd called the church and confirmed that the sanctuary would be available, and asked the Abernathy's to perform the ceremony. Once he'd cleared everything with Bobbi, the plan had been set in motion. He'd solicited the services of Ciara and Mackenzie to help with planning. They made sure the bride and groom had cakes, and had even secured the best soul food caterer in town for the formal dinner and reception. And thanks to Ciara, they'd used Savon's fabulous florist for Bobbi's bouquet, the decorations and centerpieces.

When the intro music for the "Cupid Shuffle" came on, Bobbi grabbed Lance by the hand and pulled him to the dance floor. Almost everyone in the room joined them, even Ava. Lil Dizzy took the mic from the DJ and became the hype man, calling out all the moves, which inspired the guests to dance harder. Thanks to Lil Dizzy's management team, they had the best DJ in Washington DC spinning tracks as a wedding gift. Every line dance created over the last ten years had played over the speakers before the night ended.

The following weekend, Ava watched Dizzy play video games in one of the guest bedrooms. After the wedding, Dizzy had asked if he could stay over for a few days and he still hadn't left. For all practical purposes, he had become a voting member of the Holder household.

As for Bobbi and Lance, they were in the final stages of planning their honeymoon. Just a few more things to work out with babysitting and their businesses and they would be set.

Rubbing Lance's head, Bobbi smiled down at her husband as he lay on her lap in their basement theater room. "Bae," she said. "Now that we're married, there's something I've been meaning to ask you." She suppressed the urge to giggle. "Why do you wear your clothes so tight?"

Lance sat up. "What do you mean?"

"Sweetie, it was the first thing I noticed about you. We have to get you some clothes that fit."

"I like showing off my muscles though." Lance stretched out his arm and curled it twice. "See. Feel that gun," he said.

"Yes, babe. Good job." Bobbi patted his muscle. "But you need to have a little wiggle room in your shirts and jackets. You know— just in case you need to lift your arms or tie your shoe, or drive, or bend your elbow to eat, or use your computer, or brush your hair—" she muttered.

Wrinkles formed on Lance's brow. "Ha ha—very funny." Lance looked at his arm, noticing for the first time just how tight the short-sleeved shirt was around it. He chuckled. "If you think I need bigger clothes . . . I trust your judgment." He pulled her to him. "Now, give your man some love."

Bobbi kissed her husband. "Great! I'll take you shopping before we leave for London." *Whew . . . thank you, Jesus.*

From the Author

Dear Reader,

I hope you were entertained by Bobbi's story. Writing about the oh-so-familiar struggles many singles face, especially woman, gets me excited. But there was a greater purpose.

Real life happens to everyone—even Christians. Many single Christians are challenged with abstinence because they want to be in loving, meaningful relationships. But how does abstaining even work if you're not a virgin, right?

I would imagine that a great number of singles find themselves in similar situations to Bobbi's and Savon's, with no one to talk to about it. Not everyone has a Sister Ruth on speed dial.

The topic of sex can no longer be taboo for the Church at large. There are more singles sitting in the pews at most services than there are married couples. Singles need somewhere to go to be heard, to cry, to be healed, to be encouraged, to be ministered to without judgment, and to know that forgiveness is possible. That place should be the Church.

If this story resonated with your own, on any level, please know that God cares about you and what you're going through. His love is ferocious toward you. And as this same unstoppable love upholds the universe, so will it also uphold you. Believe it!

Much love,
Vanessa

Visit Vanessa on the Web:
VanessaWerts.com
Twitter @VanessaWerts
Facebook.com/AuthorVanessaWerts

CPSIA information can be obtained
at www.ICGtesting.com
Printed in the USA
FSOW02n1435011116
26845FS